PRAISE F(

MW01004516

"David Desmond has written a hilarious tale based on his insider's knowledge of life in Palm Beach and Paris. It should be a big success."

Donald Trump

"Can we talk? *The Misadventures of Oliver Booth* is filled with intimate details about the you-know-whos doing you-know-what in Palm Beach and Paris. You're going to love it! It's a fast and fun read."

Joan Rivers

"A hilarious and sweet satire of Palm Beach so-called society, sprinkled with an equally critical and amusing look at the world of antiques. A must, fun read, even more so if you like Paris or wish to go!"

Florence de Dampierre
Author of *French Chic* and Other Books

"Insightful and wickedly funny, David Desmond writes with an insider's knowledge of Palm Beach society and the world of antiques. Beware of those Oliver Booths when designing your home—they do exist—and Desmond captures that persona beautifully."

Zaniz Jakubowski
Interior Designer to the Stars

"*The Misadventures of Oliver Booth* takes a lightly analytical, highly satirical look at the human flora and fauna of Palm Beach."

Alison Lurie
Pulitzer Prize-Winning Novelist

"*The Misadventures of Oliver Booth* is the perfect social satire and perfectly hilarious. We learn that great social pretension can lead to equally great disaster and one cannot help but lovingly follow the main character's slow-motion downfall. With an insider's view, David Desmond reveals the ever effervescent ins and outs of social mountaineering. Following the main character's journey from Palm Beach to Paris is like watching a beautiful car accident: Oliver Booth is the acquaintance one loves to hate and his story had us in stitches from start to finish. We certainly cannot wait for the continuation of the tale."

Bernd Dams and Andrew Zega
Authors of *Versailles, Chinoiseries*, and Other Books

"As a New Orleanian, I instantly felt like Ignatius J. Reilly of *A Confederacy of Dunces* had been reincarnated in the form of Oliver Booth. I had no idea how much I missed Ignatius until I found myself finished with the book in two sittings. Now I miss Oliver! I can only imagine what he'll get into next. Hurry, David, we're waiting!"

Ti Adelaide Martin
Proprietor of Commander's Palace Restaurant

The Misadventures of
OLIVER BOOTH
Life in the Lap of Luxury

The Misadventures of
OLIVER BOOTH
Life in the Lap of Luxury

DAVID DESMOND

GREENLEAF
BOOK GROUP PRESS

Notice: This book is a work of fiction. Names, characters, businesses, organizations, places, events, and incidents are either a product of the author's imagination or are used fictitiously. Any resemblance to actual persons, living or dead, events, or locales is entirely coincidental.

Published by Greenleaf Book Group
4425 S. Mo Pac Expressway, Suite 600
Austin, TX 78735

Copyright ©2009 David Desmond

All rights reserved under all copyright conventions. No part of this book may be reproduced, stored in a retrieval system, or transmitted by any means, electronic, mechanical, photocopying, recording, or otherwise, without written permission from the publisher.

Distributed by Greenleaf Book Group LLC
For ordering information or special discounts for bulk purchases, please contact
Greenleaf Book Group at 4425 S. Mo Pac Expressway, Suite 600, Austin, TX 78735 or
phone (512) 891-6100.

Design and composition by Greenleaf Book Group LLC
Cover design by Greenleaf Book Group LLC
Cover illustration by Carrie Kabak
Author photo by Lee Hershfield/Palm Beach Daily News

Publisher's Cataloging-in-Publication Data
(Prepared by The Donohue Group, Inc.)

Desmond, David.
    The misadventures of Oliver Booth : life in the lap of luxury / David Desmond. -- 1st ed.

    p. ; cm.

    ISBN: 978-1-929774-56-2

1. Antique dealers--Florida--Palm Beach--Fiction. 2. Upper class--Florida--Palm Beach--Fiction. 3. Shopping--France--Paris--Fiction. I. Title.

PS3604.E7595 M57 2009
813/.6   2008929353

Printed in the United States of America on acid-free paper

11 10 09 08   10 9 8 7 6 5 4 3 2 1

First edition

TO LISA AND ROBERT

Je préfère un enfer intelligent à un paradis stupide.

—Victor Hugo

PROLOGUE

Palm Beach is a 16-mile-long but very narrow island located on the southeast coast of Florida, bounded by the
Atlantic Ocean to the east and the Intracoastal Waterway to
the west. Although its year-round population of 10,000 residents is small, Palm Beach contains arguably the densest con-
centration of wealthy individuals of any municipality in the
world.

At the heart of Palm Beach lies the estate section, where
properties range in value from $2 million for a starter home
to $20 million or more for a residence of importance. Scat-
tered throughout this section are many historic houses that
reflect the distinctive architectural style of Palm Beach, with
reefs of harvested coquina and thousands upon thousands of
clay roof tiles bearing the shape and hue of bronzed Latin
thighs sheltering their privileged residents from the steamy
tropical climate. Regrettably, despite the diligent efforts of the
town fathers, the existence of these historic homes is now
being threatened—not by age or the elements but by an

onslaught of investment bankers and their trophy wives who would not hesitate to demolish them in the misguided belief that bigger must be better.

The commercial center of Palm Beach is Worth Avenue, which is located on the northern edge of the estate section and bisects the island. It consists of one long block, where all of the finest and most expensive boutiques in the world are represented. Recognizing that one's hired help would be responsible for such trivialities as shopping for groceries, collecting the dry cleaning, and taking the children and pets to the doctor, the resources of Worth Avenue would otherwise be sufficient to satisfy all of the essential needs of the residents of Palm Beach, as long as those essential needs involved only fashion and fine dining.

Most of the inhabitants of Palm Beach are in residence on a seasonal basis, choosing to spend the humid summer months in cooler northern climates. During the winter, they typically avoid leaving the island, and residents of neighboring and comparably affluent locales bemoan their inability to entice them to attend their events. Certain uncommon circumstances—a hurricane evacuation or a hospitalization for a hip replacement, for example—might cause Palm Beachers to cross one of the three bridges connecting their island to the mainland. Otherwise, leaving Palm Beach just isn't done.

PART I

PALM BEACH

CHAPTER ONE

Oliver Booth did not believe in New Year's resolutions. Instead, he felt that it was the responsibility of others to adapt to what he considered to be his minor quirks. He was wrong.

When Oliver awoke in his Palm Beach residence on the morning of his 52nd New Year's Eve, the weatherman was reporting that the temperature had already climbed to well over 80 degrees, and the increasing heat and humidity made it likely that there would be an intense thunderstorm at some point during the day. Although he had lived in Palm Beach for the last 32 years, Oliver continued to believe that it should be at least cool on New Year's Eve. Few people knew that he had spent the first 20 years of his life up north in a dismal Philadelphia neighborhood lacking in opportunity and style and far from the tony Main Line. With few prospects, Oliver had spent two years in an ill-fated effort to obtain an associate's degree in interior design. After failing Chintz Theory 101 and Remedial Gimp, Oliver decided to start a new life and seek his fortune by moving to Palm Beach to sell antiques.

Stores on Worth Avenue make a great deal of money from walk-in customers. Unfortunately for Oliver, his shop was not located on Worth Avenue. Instead, one needed to walk to the very end of the block and then turn right to find it just next door to the Seminole Men's Barbershop, which in its Old World style offered not only haircuts but also manicures, pedicures, and scalp massages to the addled elders of Palm Beach. Thus, Oliver's shop was a destination, albeit an uncommon one, requiring that customers make a conscious decision to visit, because no one ventured off Worth Avenue without a purpose.

Despite the effort required to hoist his girth up the stairs, Oliver lived in a small apartment above his shop. Visitors to his private quarters were rare, but he had nevertheless attempted to decorate his apartment in a manner befitting royalty, with excessively grand gilded furniture diverted from his downstairs inventory of Mexican reproductions of classic French designs filling every empty space. Oliver's only companion in his home was a pet, an obese French bulldog named Napoleon who was not only flatulent and dyspeptic, like Oliver, but also frequently incontinent—regrettably, often on faux Aubusson rugs. Potential clients wandering in the door were assaulted by the cloud of noxious fumes that surrounded the beast, but Oliver had become acclimated to the odor. Given that Oliver refused to spend money on advertising in any of the popular Palm Beach periodicals, he spent a great deal of his time lacking in human company, consoling himself instead with the affections of Napoleon.

Oliver believed that impeccable grooming and fashionable dress were the keys to a dealer's success in the world of antiques. During hot days—typically ten months of the year—he wore Bermuda shorts, along with the requisite knee socks and Italian loafers. His shirts were also Italian and silk, and he rotated through a collection of sport coats in pink, yellow, lime green, and sea foam, as well as dark blue for formal occasions. Oliver always wore a tie with a matching pocket square, which tended to be far more flamboyant than was considered appropriate in Palm Beach.

To complete his look, Oliver heavily accessorized his outfits with jewelry, including large gold pinky rings on each hand. Of course, in the intense heat of Palm Beach, even the best of men cannot help but perspire, and Oliver tended to refresh his cologne throughout the day in order to combat his tendency to stink. One unintended benefit of his use of these excessive amounts of cologne was that his scent partially compensated for that of Napoleon.

Oliver's office was located at the back of his shop. Scattered around his desk were the many popular magazines that he consulted to keep himself current on the trials and tribulations of the numerous B- and C-level celebrities who congregated seasonally in Palm Beach. Each issue was well read and usually stained with food. Photos of Oliver with certain of the more questionable celebrities were pinned to a corkboard in front of his desk, along with unpaid invoices, inspirational quotes, daily affirmations, and a list of the telephone numbers of the few regular clients that he still maintained.

When intermittent social obligations with persons who had no alternative arose, Oliver relied on clerks to supervise his shop. This was not truly necessary because days often went by without a single customer gracing his doorstep. Oliver enjoyed his role as an authority figure, however, and it would be reasonable to assume that he hired clerks more to receive his abuse than to receive his clients.

Few clerks could tolerate Oliver for more than a month. After having been pushed to the breaking point, they would flee the shop weeping and flinging verbal epithets and, sometimes, small pieces of furniture. The more resourceful and perhaps vengeful of these former clerks would set traps for Oliver just prior to their departure. One clerk replaced Oliver's snuff with hot pepper flakes, while another sawed off the bottom three inches of each of the legs of his desk chair, causing Oliver to feel diminished, at least in the physical sense.

Oliver's most recent hire, an unfortunate young person named Schmidt, had started working at the shop only three days previously, but the demands of the job would soon cause him to be seeking new employment. As the clock approached noon on New Year's Eve day, Oliver descended the stairs from his apartment to begin his typically brief working day.

"Come here, Schmidt," he said. "Tell me, has the mail arrived?"

"Yes, Oliver."

Oliver looked at Schmidt with an expression of horror and outrage. "How many times have I told you, call me Mr. Booth or sir, is that clear?"

"Yes, I'm sorry."

"Alright, who am I?"

"You are Mr. Booth."

"Who?"

"Mr. Booth, sir."

"Better. Try to concentrate on your work. The well-heeled residents of this community are relying on us to fashion their environments and we will not let them down. Now review the mail for me."

Schmidt picked up a stack of envelopes, catalogs, and magazines and began to flip through them.

"Tell me about each item. Begin with the magazines."

"Alright, here is *Hello* magazine—"

"And who is on the cover?"

"Someone called Tara Palmer-Tomkinson. I haven't heard of her."

"Of course you haven't heard of her. People like Tara Palmer-Tomkinson do not associate with people like you." Oliver had never heard of Tara Palmer-Tomkinson either. "Move on, next magazine."

"Alright, the next magazine is the spring issue of the *Affluent Enthusiast*. That's not a very informative name, is it? The cover has a photo of a watch and the lead story is entitled 'Bejeweled Timepieces: Measuring Luxury by the Second.'"

"Ah, the *Affluent Enthusiast*. *The* manual for comfortable living. Fine. Next."

"Your last magazine is a complimentary copy of *The Economist*. Would you like me to—"

"*Boring.* Move on to the letters."

Schmidt dropped the stack of magazines and catalogs on Oliver's desk and sat down on a reproduction of a Louis the Fourteenth armchair.

"Do not sit on the products. You will soil them and make them unsaleable. Stand and review my mail."

Schmidt opened an envelope. "The first letter is from Florida Power and Light. It says that you owe them $2,756.43 for the last five months of service."

"Air-conditioning is expensive in this godforsaken climate. I must keep Napoleon comfortable and maintain the quality of the products that we are displaying."

"Mr. Booth, since most of our products are made in Mexico, wouldn't they be used to the heat?"

"You fool, they are not '*our*' products, they are '*my*' products, and their provenance is none of your business. Next letter!"

"Um, the Worth Avenue Merchants Association has sent you a letter of complaint. Apparently, Napoleon defecated in front of the restaurant Ta-boó during the lunch hour. The letter states that this is not the first time this has happened and that if it happens again, they will be forced to suspend your membership. And they remind you that you still haven't paid this year's dues."

"Screw them all. Would they prefer that Napoleon be constipated? He was simply performing a natural bodily function. And I'll send in my dues when I'm good and ready. How many more letters are there?"

"Three more, and they're all stamped 'Past Due.' Let's see, the first letter is from VB Holdings regarding your rent. The second letter—"

"That's enough. I'll deal with them later. Just get back to work. Your next task will be to stack those antique Portuguese tiles in order of width."

"Mr. Booth, I wanted to ask you whether I might be able to leave a little early today since you had me work through my lunch hour yesterday. Perhaps at 4:00 p.m.? And, by the way, I think those tiles are from Mexico."

"You ungrateful fool! You should thank me for providing you with your tasks. You can't even imagine how much you might learn from a person like me."

"But I just thought—"

"You haven't had a thought in your entire life, you slacker. You're fired!"

"But—"

"Go now. I'm sure they're looking for stock boys at Publix."

And that's how Oliver Booth caused himself to be clerkless on New Year's Eve.

* * *

At the Morningwood Club, the afternoon tea of the Dowagers in Paradise, an exclusive social group that included only the wealthiest divorcées, was drawing to a close. As they rose to leave, the DIPs, as they were known by the club staff—and, actually, everyone in Palm Beach—were slightly unsteady on their feet due to their having spontaneously added six bottles of pinot grigio to their high tea menu. Despite the heat, the postprandial letdown, and their apparent instability, however, these women never appeared less than fully alert, much like meerkats on the African veld, owing to repeated but decreasingly successful cosmetic procedures involving their faces and necks. The DIPs were far beyond the age at which Botox could even be considered, and each woman was nearing the point at which nothing short of a face transplant would be able to improve her appearance.

The denouements of these teas were always tense because each of the women wanted to demonstrate her fiscal superiority by picking up the check, but none of them actually wanted to pay the bill. One might guess that this penurious nature was a gesture of respect toward their departed husbands' years of diligent effort to build their fortunes. In fact, most of these women had become divorcées long before the deaths of their husbands and they were simply acting on their desire to protect the proceeds of the impressive divorce settlements that each of them had obtained.

Perhaps a parallel tea was being held that included all of the trophy wives of those deceased moneyed men, whose sexual gymnastics and spending habits had put their husbands in a slightly early grave. That parallel tea would have been taking place in South Beach, however, and each of those trophy widows would have had only her Cuban fitness instructor on her mind as she departed the restaurant.

The ostensible leader of the DIPs was Margaret Van Buren, the doyenne of the Palm Beach social scene. She was "of a certain age," as they say, that age being 73, but she had avoided the cosmetic procedures that had left the remaining DIPs in a state of suspended animation. Despite 20 extra pounds and a gray bouffant hairdo from a bygone era, it could be said that Mrs. Van Buren had aged gracefully, an outcome facilitated by a very long, very happy, and very luxurious marriage to her husband, Mickey Van Buren, who had made his fortune manufacturing explosives. Upon his peaceful passing, he had left her an estate valued at $500 million, which included one of the largest, most beautiful, and most important homes in Palm Beach.

In addition to her grandson, Martin, whom she was helping to raise, and her butler, James, Mrs. Van Buren's only year-round companion in her home was her three-pound dog, a Yorkshire terrier bitch known as Champion Dame Agatha the Superbad Yakuza in dog show circles and Daisy everywhere else. Daisy was with Mrs. Van Buren during this luncheon with the DIPs; in fact, it was only on rare occasions that she was seen sitting anywhere other than on her owner's lap.

Mrs. Van Buren had mixed feelings about the DIPs, in part because she was a widow rather than a divorcée. Although she was heavily involved in charitable works, she certainly did not need their financial support, but she did require their physical presence at the various events that she chaired. The DIPs cast a wide social net, and each would be sure to drag many friends along to fill the tables that she had purchased for the endless succession of gala evenings that were held throughout the season. For that reason, Mrs. Van Buren willingly hosted these high teas, although for the most part, the conversation tended to be tedious.

The comments of the DIPs were forgettable for their vapidity. Marylou Adams was typical. She had been telling her fellow DIPs about a meeting that she had had with her interior designer regarding the redecoration of her home and mentioned that he had shown her a photograph of a George the Third center table for her foyer that had been priced at $9,000. She told her friends that she had been shocked.

"'Darling,' I told him, 'the table is lovely, but I was hoping for something a little more expensive.'"

The women tittered with recognition, believing that the sole purpose of interior design was to impress one's friends. Regrettably for them, the displaying of price tags had never come into vogue.

"I mean, really, how could I possibly be expected to appreciate the beauty of something so . . . *inexpensive?*"

Many heads nodded in unison.

Mrs. Van Buren arched an eyebrow. "But Marylou, wouldn't you agree that it would be possible, hypothetically speaking, to decorate an entire room for, say, $10,000?"

Mrs. Adams looked at her blankly. "I don't understand. How could that be possible? Ten thousand dollars wouldn't even pay for the curtains."

Mrs. Van Buren looked slightly annoyed. "My point is that beauty is not a function of price. I mean, you can buy expensive things that are beautiful, but it's also possible to find beauty in things that are inexpensive. Look at these flowers, for example." She reached out and touched the petals of a white orchid that was standing in a vase on the table. "Orchids are so inexpensive here in Florida, but their subtlety and complexity and absolute beauty cannot be questioned."

Mrs. Adams frowned. "Oh, Margaret, don't be so naïve. Those orchids are not inexpensive. First, to be able to reach out and touch them, you need to be welcome at the high tea of the Dowagers of Paradise.

"Second, to be a member of the Dowagers, you need to be a member of Morningwood.

"Third, to be a member of Morningwood, you need to have a lot of money.

"Fourth, to have a lot of money, at least in the case of the women at this table, you need to have been married to a man who made a lot of money."

Mrs. Adams batted her eyelashes in an unsuccessful effort to appear coy and then she continued. "And fifth, you would have had to have divorced that man and received sufficient funds in the divorce settlement to support this lifestyle. So, that orchid is not inexpensive. It comes at an extremely high emotional cost to all of us. Plus, think of all of the times we had to look at our ex-husbands naked." She wrinkled her nose with distaste.

Mrs. Van Buren sighed. "Well, as you all know, I am a widow, not a divorcée, so I cannot share all of your feelings, but I think it's quite possible, and necessary, to make an effort to see the beauty in everything around you, regardless of its price. Conversely, it's also important to be able to recognize the ugliness in people and things, because that will enhance your understanding of beauty. But after all of that pinot grigio, I can see that this discussion is getting to be a bit too cerebral for you. I believe it's time to conclude our festivities. I'm sure many of us need to begin preparing for tonight's New Year's Eve party."

* * *

Private clubs are at the heart of Palm Beach culture. Unlike the Mar-a-Lago Club, the Bath and Tennis Club, and the Everglades Club, however, Morningwood could be considered to be second tier at best. Its membership was sought only by those who were socially inept or under indictment, and the only criteria for admittance were extreme wealth and the proper religious affiliation. Standing in contrast to the general membership was Margaret Van Buren, the daughter of the club's founder. She remained an active member of the club out of respect for her father, but much to her regret she no longer retained any formal power to influence its everyday functioning.

Morningwood required a staff of 243 to function properly. Unfortunately, its staff numbered only 132, which resulted in much frantic scurrying about as its human resources were continually reallocated to meet the changing demands of the day. Morningwood also relied on a stream of new job applicants to compensate for the ceaseless exodus of employees who had been fired after trivial indiscretions or who had quit due to the harshly punitive nature of the club's management.

Bernard Dauphin had recently discovered the club through its job posting in the *International Herald Tribune* and he had decided to become one of those new applicants.

Bernard had grown up in the town of Aix-en-Provence in southeastern France. At 21, after having completed a three-year program at the Université de Provence, where he had specialized in English, he had made up his mind to take a little time off, see the world, and—he hoped—make a little money along the way. Bernard had the crooked nose, protruding ears, and naturally tousled black hair of a young Serge Gainsbourg. For some reason, young women tended to find those features quite appealing, but, unlike that slightly disheveled louche French singer, Bernard gravitated toward carefully pressed dark suits, white shirts, and narrow ties, and he never displayed anything less than impeccable manners.

On the afternoon of December 31st, Bernard found himself sitting in the office of the club manager, Earl Perch. Mr. Perch was a good (very) old boy who had been managing Morningwood for 45 years, and he was uncomfortable with and irritated by people who were unlike himself. That would include anyone who was a woman, other than Caucasian, other than Protestant, other than American, other than 70-plus years of age, and other than Earl Perch. The interview began inauspiciously.

"Do . . . you . . . speak . . . English?"

"Yes, fluently," replied Bernard. "I specialized in English as part of my baccalaureate and later at the Université de Provence."

"Were you trying to keep that a secret?"

"What do you mean?"

"Well, Bernie, you wrote here that you're French."

"Yes, well, my name is Bernard, actually, and it's true that I am from France, but I studied English formally for a number of years. I also lived in New York between the ages of 12 and 16 while my father attended the Executive Program at the Cornell School of Hotel Administration and then worked as a manager at the Plaza Hotel, so I am now fluent in your language."

Perch was pensive. "What makes you think you can understand the needs of my club members? These bastards are rich and they can be very demanding. I mean, you're *French*."

"I will try to be sensitive to their needs, monsieur."

"What? What's that word you said?"

"Sensitive?"

"No, no, the last word, son!"

"Uh, monsieur?"

"That's it! That's perfect! Okay, I'm gonna give you a job as a French waiter. The members will eat up that French act."

"It's not an act. Truly, I am from France."

"I don't give a damn, boy. Just call them all monsieur and madame and whatever else you can think up that sounds classy, bring them whatever they want, and then get the hell out of their way. You should be fine. Report to Mr. Helmut König, the catering manager, and he'll get you set up with a uniform and some training. He's Austrian, so you'll get along fine. You French like working for the Austrians, right?"

"Well, I—"

"And get a crew cut. It works for me. I'm sick of all these hippies running around talking about peace and love, with their hair touching their collar."

"Mr. Perch, I take pride in my appearance," replied Bernard. "I promise you that it will be satisfactory."

Perch inspected Bernard from across his desk. "Hmm, well, I suppose you do look relatively clean-cut. Alright, forget the crew cut, but you WILL bathe more than once a week. You're in America now, boy!"

* * *

Helmut König had been raised in the mountains of southwestern Argentina in a lakeside town called Bariloche to which his family had immigrated from Austria following the "difficulties" of 1945. He had been happy in Bariloche, which felt like a little piece of the Alps that had been transplanted into South America, and he had accepted the need to wear lederhosen and a felt cap as the price of success as he moved up the ranks at the Enrique Himmler chocolate factory.

An economic downturn in the 1990s had caused the candy industry to collapse in Argentina, however, and König had decided that he would take advantage of his accent and his continental charm by seeking employment in the American hospitality industry. As the catering manager of Morningwood, he ruled the club's employees with an iron fist, but he preferred to delegate training activities to his underlings. He deigned to train Bernard only because he was short staffed.

"So, Bernhard, you are French, *ja?*"

"Actually, Mr. König, my name is Bernard, and, yes, I am from Aix-en-Provence."

"Ah, Aix-en-Provence. I have never been there, but my father told me stories about hiking through there as a youth in 1940. He and his friends walked all the way from Bregenz to Aix-en-Provence and then to Paris, where they lived for four years. He told me that he had enjoyed meeting many local people and that the French had bent over backward to take care of him while he lived in Paris. Do you have a similar interest in taking care of our members? May I give you a little test to see if you know anything?"

"Of course, I think I will do well."

"Fine. We will see. First, a little quiz. What is an Arnold Palmer?"

"Isn't Arnold Palmer a golfer?"

"Yes, of course, but what is *an* Arnold Palmer?"

"A very good golfer?"

"No, you fool, an Arnold Palmer is a popular beverage. It is half iced tea and half lemonade. Not a very promising start, eh, my young French friend?"

"Well, now I know."

"Next question. What is a spritzer?"

"I'm not sure."

"You may take a guess."

"Um, is it something that sprays water on the grass when it hasn't rained?"

"No, no, that's a sprinkler, dummkopf! A spritzer is another beverage that is part wine and part club soda. So, beverages are not your strong suit. I'll have you spend some time with the bartender and you'll pick up these terms quickly."

König handed Bernard a menu and a wine list. "Look, I don't have time for this. Tonight is the most important night of the year, New Year's Eve. Memorize the dinner menu and the wine list. You will work in the main dining room tonight. We should be able to find you a uniform that will fit. Give the members attitude and speak with a heavy French accent. They'll like that. They'll think it's a sign of class."

Bernard watched König walk off toward the spa and thought, "Perhaps I should have taken that job in Sardinia."

CHAPTER TWO

The gala New Year's Eve party at the Morningwood Club was always the most expensive evening of the year. At a cost of $1,000 per person, members and their guests would enjoy cocktails and caviar beginning at 7:00, a five-course dinner beginning at 8:00, and then a show featuring a fading celebrity beginning at 10:00 and running through the magical hour of midnight. Oliver arrived at 6:30 in the hope of staking out a position at the caviar display and getting a head start. Familiar with this strategy, the staff asked him to wait outside until the appointed hour.

Attired in a deep-blue crushed velvet smoking jacket with a shawl collar, heavily pleated black pants tenuously supported by suspenders, and beribboned black patent leather loafers, Oliver stood outside the club entrance, stewing angrily in the moist heat. Due to recent indulgences, which dwarfed his past indulgences, Oliver's waistline had been expanding. As a result, all of his clothes had become even more formfitting, particularly this outfit, which he had not worn since the preceding New Year's Eve. His puffy jowls strained the delicate threads of his collar, and his clip-on bow tie threatened to burst from his throat at any moment. The lowest of the three buttons on his paisley vest had already popped off, leaving only two to restrain his corpulent belly.

Oliver spotted the club receptionist walking toward the employee smoking area. He hauled himself over to her, sweating even more profusely with the effort, and attempted to press a damp $20 bill into her hand.

"Ah, Melanie, you look lovely tonight. Please allow me to thank you in advance for ensuring that I will be seated at an entertaining table. Tell me, will Mrs. Van Buren be attending the festivities?"

"Yes, Mr. Booth, she will be here, but her table is already complete. Seven of her friends will be joining her."

Oliver offered his most ingratiating smile. "I wonder if there is any chance that you could see your way clear to include one additional chair at the table? I'm just a waif, as you can see!"

Melanie looked down at the protruding belly and then looked up to see Oliver's red, sweaty, grinning face. "Mr. Booth," she said, "I'm so sorry, but there is no way we could add another seat to an already full table, and Mrs. Van Buren would need to approve the inclusion of any additional guests anyway. She is our wealthiest member, you know. I don't recall exactly where you've been seated, but I'm sure you will find it to be more than satisfactory."

Oliver contemplated ways that he might retrieve his $20 bill but quickly decided that he would simply write off its loss as a business expense.

Noticing Oliver's disheartened expression, Melanie looked at her watch and said, "Mr. Booth, it's almost 7:00 now and I'm sure it wouldn't be a problem for you to go in."

* * *

Oliver was the first guest to enter the club. Although the patio on which the cocktail party would be taking place looked quite empty, this in no way dissuaded him from trundling over to the caviar bar, planting his meaty legs, and picking up three small cocktail plates, regretting only that he had been provided with a small serving spoon rather than a shovel.

The salty fishiness of the caviar, as well as a desire to make the most of his very expensive ticket, caused Oliver to develop a craving for champagne, preferably very expensive champagne. He began waving his hand in the air in an effort to attract a server's attention. Bernard had been passing by, and much to his misfortune, he spotted Oliver and walked over to see if he could be of assistance.

"Listen, bring me a glass of good champagne," said Oliver. "This caviar is very salty and it's making me thirsty."

"Monsieur, if you would look to your left, you will find an attended bar that I'm sure will be able to provide you with very good champagne," replied Bernard.

Oliver scowled. "Perhaps you didn't understand me," he said. "Let me make myself clear. I asked YOU to bring ME a glass of champagne. I did not ask for directions. I am hot, I am sweaty, I am thirsty, and I am NOT leaving this spot because I am going to continue to eat as much of this beluga caviar as I can stuff down my throat until dinner begins. Now go!"

Bernard permitted Oliver to maintain his illusion that he was eating beluga caviar rather than the far less expensive Mississippi River hackleback caviar that he had actually been served. Having been taught that the American service motto was "The customer is always right," apparently even when he is an idiot (in place of the French service motto "The customer is always an idiot," even when he isn't), Bernard walked the three feet to the bar and requested a glass of champagne.

Eric the bartender-singer-dancer-actor-escort, who had worked at the club during the preceding three seasons, asked, "Is the champagne for that sweaty fellow over there?"

"Yes."

"I've dealt with him before. He's such a hog. Here, give this to him and get the hell out of his way. Feel free to thank me later."

"I'll thank you now, actually," said Bernard. "I appreciate the advice."

Bernard carried a glass of the excessively fizzing liquid over to Oliver, who received it with a grunt and a sneer. Because of the high price of champagne, and despite the high price that the club was charging for the evening's festivities, it had been decided that the guests would instead be served Sueur d'Aisselle, a sparkling wine of recent vintage from upstate New York. The Sueur d'Aisselle had been transferred into bottles of Dom Perignon that had been emptied by the club's administrators at their Christmas party the preceding week, however, so Oliver and the other members would be none the wiser.

Bernard reflected that this had been a very inauspicious beginning to his new job and contemplated calling his travel agent the following day to book a flight to Sardinia. That busboy position at Cala di Volpe was looking awfully good.

* * *

Seating for dinner began at 7:45. At 7:30, Oliver had taken the liberty of sneaking into the ballroom. Having discovered that Mrs. Van Buren and her party would, of course, be seated at Table 1, he had added a place setting and a seat to an already full table. By the time Mrs. Van Buren and her guests arrived a few minutes before 8:00, escorted by Helmut König and Melanie, Oliver had wedged himself into a seat, where they found him looking up like an expectant puppy.

Melanie took the initiative. "Oh, Mr. Booth, I'm sure you must remember that I told you that there is no room at Mrs. Van Buren's table for any additional, unapproved guests. I must ask you, please, to see one of my assistants who would be happy to look up the number of your own table."

Oliver was distraught. "Dear Mrs. Van Buren, you must remember me. I'm Oliver Booth. I sell fine antiques on Worth Avenue. So many of my customers are your closest friends, and I thought tonight would be a wonderful opportunity for us to get to know each other."

Mrs. Van Buren strained her neck to look toward the ceiling, doing her best to avoid Oliver's gaze while allowing Melanie to do the dirty work.

"Mr. Booth, please, I must ask you, once again, to move from this table to your assigned seat. Thank you in advance for your cooperation."

Oliver, mortified, stood up and stepped away. Finding an assistant nearby with a seating chart, he gave her his name and skulked behind her as she led him to his table. It was quite a long walk from Table 1, and, as they neared the rear exit, Oliver asked, "Excuse me, why are we leaving the ballroom?"

"We're not leaving, sir, I'm leading you to your table. Ah, here we are, Table 97. Have a Happy New Year!"

"Wait, there must be some mistake," said Oliver. "This table is against the back wall of the ballroom and there's only one seat."

"Oh no, sir, there's no mistake. Tables toward the front of the ballroom are reserved for groups that have asked to be seated together. Since you have no friends, uh, guests, we could not take the liberty of placing you at a table with seven strangers. I'm sure you'll be much more comfortable here with this wonderful table all to yourself. Think about it, you won't need to make small talk for the next four hours! How lucky you are! Bye now! Have fun!"

Oliver stood there wearing a look of horror as the assistant departed. He collapsed into the single seat, the impact causing him to emit a loud belch that resulted from the pile of hackleback caviar he had just consumed.

"This will not do," thought Oliver. "It simply will not do."

But Oliver's evening would only get worse.

* * *

The primary advantage of working as a waiter on New Year's Eve lay in the set menu. Every club member, excluding certain belligerent vegans—who were typically younger guests of club members rather than club members themselves—and those unfortunate persons who were allergic to nuts and other more far-fetched food items, would be served the same four-course meal.

Already plated when guests were seated was an *amuse bouche* of salmon mousse on a toast point. A very pedestrian effort, but it was hoped that the inclusion of salmon would be considered classy. Also, those club members who had heard of an amuse bouche had been taught to believe that it was a complimentary item provided through the good graces of the chef. Of course, at a dinner priced at $1,000 per plate, nothing is complimentary, and the cost of that small portion of salmon mousse was probably closer to $50.

Next, the guests were to be served a salad that consisted of half a head of iceberg lettuce and one slice of tomato wallowing in a pool of Russian dressing. Perhaps in the food trade this would be considered "checking the box." Choosing the most rudimentary of salads to serve as the salad course? Check.

The entrée for the evening was a carnivore's delight, consisting as it did of a small filet mignon, a small lamb chop, and a small piece of veal, all of which were overcooked due to the need to prepare them early on such a busy evening and keep them warming over Sterno pots. To round out the dish with the requisite vegetable and starch, the guests were presented with a decorative clamshell filled with creamed spinach and a small mound of mashed potatoes.

The dessert was a slice of flourless *ganache* cake with the texture of extruded latex resting in a thin pool of mango-jalapeño sauce. As the guests quickly discovered, the first bite yielded a sensation akin to being struck on the tongue with a chocolate sledgehammer, and the potent flavors of the cake and the sauce battled each other like two socialites fighting over the last pair of size 38s at a Blahnik sample sale. Even for the culinary hedonists in the crowd, it was a bit much.

All in all, this was a predictable and ultimately unsatisfying gastronomic experience, much as the club members had been trained to expect during so many similar events in the past.

* * *

Bernard approached Helmut König to inquire about his duties that evening. He was told to find his table assignments on the seating chart attached to the wall leading into the kitchen. Bernard had been assigned seven tables, numbers 91 through 97. This was quite a large number, actually, given that he had only begun working at the club a few hours previously.

Bernard proceeded to take drink orders from Tables 91 through 96 in rapid succession, his efforts speeded by the placement of large open bottles of house red and white wine on each table before the guests were seated. He then moved toward Table 97, where, to his horror, he discovered that the pudgy, demanding man from earlier in the evening was sitting. By himself.

"Good evening again, monsieur. For some reason, you are missing seven place settings at your table. Please give me just a few minutes and I'll do my best to make sure that your table is properly set before your guests arrive."

"Listen, boob, there will be no guests, and stop calling me monsieur. I was seated here against my will and I am mortified. I feel like a leper and I am being bruised by the swing of the kitchen door."

Oliver reached inside his smoking jacket and extracted his wallet. "I'll make a deal with you," he said. "I'll forget how you mistreated me earlier and I'll even give you $20 if you find me a seat at another table. Any other table, it doesn't matter, as long as some living, breathing people are already seated there. Which might not be so easy to find at this old-age home."

"I'm so sorry, sir, but all of the tables that I have been assigned are full. Perhaps if there are some walk-ins I could

direct them toward your available seats. Would that be helpful?"

"You must be new here, otherwise you would know that
this and every other New Year's Eve party in Palm Beach has
been sold out for months. So there aren't going to be any
walk-ins. Alright, I'm going to go outside and have a cigarette.
Do me a favor and bring me another one of those amuse
bouche things. I'm starving, and one of them really didn't
make a dent."

"Of course, sir. May I have your account number?"

"My account number? Why?"

"I'm required to charge guests for any special requests,
including second servings of any food."

"What! That's outrageous! After I paid all of that money
to attend this dinner? Absolutely not!" Oliver scowled and
mumbled to himself, "I suppose I must subsist on the food
that has already been allocated. Perhaps I will consider tonight
as the beginning of my diet." He looked up to find that Bernard had been listening to him and added hastily, "Not that I
need to diet, mind you, but it's good for the soul now and
then to deprive oneself."

Bernard reflected that a rigorous diet and perhaps a good
flogging would be beneficial for this bloated, belligerent man,
although jaw wiring and stomach stapling might have been a
more effective alternative. He cleared the single empty plate
in anticipation of the forthcoming salad course as Oliver
walked away from the table.

* * *

Oliver exited the ballroom and stepped out onto the loggia
and into the steamy Palm Beach night. He once again began

to sweat profusely, a process that was exacerbated by his outfit, which contained not a single natural fiber and thus not a single entry point for any form of ventilation.

Oliver approached one of the tall cocktail tables arrayed around the main swimming pool and reached inside his jacket for his cigarettes. He preferred to smoke extremely long, extremely slender cigarettes in the belief that the narrower the cigarette, the less chance there would be for the hazardous chemicals contained in the tobacco to find their way into his lungs. He also recognized that cultivating an effete image would help him in his business, because a macho antiques dealer would have no credibility.

An elderly, stooped club member and his very young, very blond, very buxom trophy wife approached Oliver. The wife held out her unlit, unfiltered cigarette to Oliver, prominently displaying her quail's egg of an engagement ring, and asked him for a light. As she took her first puff, her husband, feeling obligated to make small talk due to Oliver's assistance, asked, "So, young man, do you have any New Year's resolutions?"

Oliver reflected for a moment. He certainly didn't have any resolutions, but he saw in the elderly man the same thing that his wife had seen in him—that is, money. So he calibrated his supposed resolutions accordingly.

"Well, it may sound funny to you, but I have an addiction that is troubling me, and it's an addiction that is incurable. I am addicted to beautiful things. I have a shop on Worth Avenue and I sell fine antiques, but I love my products so much that I can only bear to sell them to people who share my appreciation of their beauty. And when I find such people, it troubles me to say that I will sell these products for prices that are obscenely low because I long to see them placed in homes where they will be loved."

The elderly man shifted the conversation. "I love beautiful things too, but nothing tops my wife. She looks pretty great, huh? Who would have thought a guy like me would end up with a doll like her? I'm really lucky that she's able to look past our age difference to see how much we have in common. Right, baby?"

"That's right, precious," she cooed while looking away distractedly.

"It's too bad we didn't meet 30 years ago when I was at the top of my profession. You would have been really impressed if you had seen me then, sweetheart. But 30 years ago, you would have been a fetus. And I think that would have been illegal, huh?" The elderly man nudged Oliver with his elbow and winked.

Oliver ignored the man's prodding elbow and continued. "Are you happy with your table for dinner?"

"Oh yes, Bunny and I are sitting with three other couples. We're at Table 2. I'm sure we would have been at Table 1 if Mrs. Van Buren hadn't been here."

"Really, well, I'm sure Table 2 is a very nice table," replied Oliver, who then muttered under his breath, "I'm also sure that it's a lot better than Table 97." Oliver remembered the purpose of their conversation. "Please, if you ever need any fine antiques, don't hesitate to call me. My name is Oliver Booth, and my shop is called Le Magasin du Roi Soleil."

"Is that French? What does that mean?"

"The Shop of the Sun King."

"The Shop of the Sun King? You think you're the Sun King? You're no Sun King."

"I chose that name because the antiques that I sell are from the era of the Sun King, Louis the Fourteenth. I read all about him in a magazine article."

"You said your store's on Worth Avenue? I don't remember an antique store on Worth Avenue by that name. Is it near Ta-boó?"

"Well, it's not actually on Worth Avenue, it's just around the corner at the very end of Worth Avenue."

"Oh, well, I don't go there. There's no need."

"But please consider stopping by. As I said, I'm addicted to beautiful things, and I can already tell that you have the sensibility to convince me to make you quite a deal!"

"No. I know what I know and I like what I like. I'm 88 years old, and I'm not going to begin shopping at some crazy store off Worth Avenue if I don't want to. Now, if you'll excuse us, I believe the next course is being served."

Much to Oliver's dismay, he learned that even frail elderly men have a certain amount of leverage, if not strength. As the man and his wife squeezed between Oliver and the cocktail table to proceed into the ballroom, Oliver was thrown off what one would have thought was his very low center of gravity. Regrettably, this occurred while he was standing just inches from the edge of the pool. He teetered and then toppled, and an enormous splash drew everyone's attention as he hit the water.

Oliver's pitiful skills as a swimmer were further compromised by his formfitting formal attire. A number of staff members immediately recognized the seriousness of the situation and leaped into the pool. With their concerted efforts, they were able to haul Oliver into the shallow end.

As he sat in the kiddie section of the pool, surrounded by inflatable toys and observed by a crowd of guests that had been drawn by the commotion, Oliver reflected that his evening had already ended and all he had gotten for his $1,000 had been the world's most expensive amuse bouche.

Chapter Three

The *Shiny Sheet* is the newspaper of record in Palm Beach. It covers society weddings and deaths, fashion, and local news, and many of its pages are devoted to advertisements for real estate. On New Year's Day, the paper permits its readers to live vicariously through the participants at all of the major parties that had been thrown on the preceding evening. And so it happened that Oliver recognized a full-color photograph of himself in dripping-wet evening attire on the front page of the *Shiny Sheet* on the morning of January first.

"Oh no!"

Oliver was aghast. He had not seen a photographer, but he hadn't seen much of anything, really, after he had fallen into the pool. He had wanted to wring himself out like a mop, but instead, that French waiter had escorted him to the staff locker room and waited while he changed out of his evening clothes and into one of the extra uniforms that had not been used that night. Unfortunately for Oliver, he had not noticed that a name badge was still attached to the lapel of the uniform, and he had had to undergo the indignity of being asked for a cocktail by a club member as he walked from the staff locker room to his car. He recalled that the waiter had told him that the club would be unable to refund the price of his ticket despite the unfortunate events of the evening, but that he would be pleased to have Oliver's outfit dry-cleaned and then delivered to his antique shop.

There would be no way to neutralize the impact of that photograph, though. In season, every resident of Palm Beach of any importance read the *Shiny Sheet* on a daily basis, particularly special issues devoted to major events like New Year's Eve parties. Someone once said that any publicity was good publicity, but that certainly wasn't true when it involved a position of importance, such as the brokering of antiques, when the credibility of the dealer was often sufficient to make or break a sale.

Oliver was disheartened to find a story below the photograph recounting the previous night's events. Under the headline "Obese Drunkard, Others, Tumble into the New Year," the story read:

At Morningwood last night, a man identified by club staff as a Mr. Oliver Boot, apparently a shopkeeper of some sort here in town, welcomed in the New Year by tumbling into the Blue Grotto, the club's main swimming pool. Club staff had earlier observed Mr. Boot, who is obese, consuming excessive quantities of champagne and acting in an agitated fashion, and they suggested that acute intoxication most likely played a role in his unfortunate plunge. After some minutes of struggle, complicated by his ill-fitting costume, Mr. Boot was wrestled out of the pool by two waiters, a parking valet, and a Mexican gardener. Mr. Boot was escorted from the premises without further ado.

Remarkably, in separate and unrelated incidents at the club, three additional members of Morningwood fell down flights of stairs last night. Helmut König, the catering manager, requested that the members not be identified in order to protect their privacy, but he added that such falls are quite common at Morningwood due to its festive atmosphere. "These members, they like to have a little fun," said Mr. König. "They like their champagne, their vodka, and then maybe just a little more champagne and vodka. And they don't eat! They must have hollow limbs, as you Americans like to say. But they are from some of our oldest families. I believe that one of the members who fell down the stairs last night came here on the *Mayflower!*"

"Protect their privacy indeed!" growled Oliver. "What about *my* privacy? And to suggest that I was drunk! If that old coot hadn't caused me to lose my balance, this never would have happened."

The first few notes of the "Marseillaise" sounded, signaling to Oliver that someone had entered his shop. He dropped the *Shiny Sheet* on top of his stack of unpaid bills, rose, and stepped forward into the small main showroom. It was Bernard, and he was carrying a garment bag.

"Hello, Mr. Booth. Mr. König asked me to deliver your evening clothes to you myself. He also asked me to tell you that if the smoking jacket has shrunk, it was due to the effects of the pool water and not our dry cleaning facilities."

"The jacket shrank?"

"I haven't seen it, but Mr. König mentioned that it does look a bit puckered now."

Oliver sighed. It had been difficult enough to get the jacket on *before* he fell into the pool, and it had already been let out three times previously. He might now have no choice but to purchase something roomier to replace it.

"Give it to me," he said.

Bernard handed him the garment bag and turned to leave.

"Wait, what was your name again?"

"Bernard Dauphin."

"Do I detect an accent?"

"People have suggested that I have an accent, yes."

"What kind of accent?" asked Oliver.

"Well, I'm from France, so it would be a French accent."

"Interesting." Oliver had an inspiration. "By the way, perhaps I neglected to apologize to you for my slightly irritable tone on New Year's Eve. As I'm sure you realized, the entire evening was a bit of a fiasco for me."

Bernard felt that Oliver had acted like an utter boor that night, but he remembered his position and his short tenure at the club. "It's nothing, Mr. Booth. I'm sure that I would have reacted in the same way."

"Good, my boy, very good! Please, if you have a minute, there is something I would like to discuss with you."

Bernard sat down on a gilded *fauteuil.*

"Let me begin. Do you know what you just sat on?"

"A chair?"

"Yes, of course, a chair, but what kind of chair?"

"It seems to be a copy of an old French design that has been painted gold. A very bright gold, actually."

Oliver gasped. "No! You are sitting in an armchair that was fabricated during the reign of your king Louis the

Fourteenth. It has perhaps undergone some very slight reparations."

Bernard stood up. He picked up the heavy chair and turned it over to inspect it more closely. "Then why does it say '*Hecho en Mexico*'? Doesn't that mean 'Made in Mexico'?"

"What? Give me that." Oliver grabbed the chair from him and placed it back on the floor. "Those fools, I asked them to leave that off," he muttered. "Alright, perhaps this reproduction slipped through into my stock." Oliver quickly changed his expression from irritable to ingratiating. "You seem to have a wonderful sensibility about fine furniture, young man. You know, with your accent, you could do very well in the antiques business."

"I really don't know anything about antiques, Mr. Booth."

"Do you know French history?"

"Of course. I was educated in France."

"Well, the rest you can learn, or perhaps finesse. I would like to offer you a position as my assistant. It doesn't pay very much, but you would receive a wealth of knowledge learning at my knee."

"Mr. Booth, that's certainly an unexpected, and, um, gracious offer, but, as you know, I already have a position as a waiter at the club."

"Don't you have any aspirations, boy? Do you want to be a menial your entire life?"

"Well, no," said Bernard, "but I began just recently and I was planning to—"

"Alright then. Tell me, what are your hours at the club?"

"My responsibilities change from day to day, but I anticipate that I will usually be working from 5:00 in the evening until midnight, Tuesday through Sunday, from now until the end of the season."

"That's perfect! My shop is open from noon until 5:00 every day except Sunday, Monday, and Tuesday."

"That's all?" said Bernard. "Those aren't very long hours."

"And by appointment! And by appointment! You know, I'm not running a delicatessen where anybody can just waltz on in when they feel like it. So, what do you say to my little business proposition?"

"Mr. Booth, I appreciate your kind offer, but I really don't need any extra work, and I do need to get some rest now and then."

"I know what you people are paid at the club. You're trying to tell me that you can survive on that meager salary and still have money to put away for a rainy day?"

With regret, Bernard realized that Oliver had a point. The pay at the club was low, and he wanted to be able to save some money, but it would involve working for this unpleasant person in a trade that he knew nothing about. On the other hand, this opportunity had fallen into his lap.

"How much would I be paid?"

"Oh, we can discuss that later, my boy. I'm sure you'll find it to be satisfactory. Now, it's a little after noon and you won't be needed at the club for five hours. Why don't you begin your new position right away by helping me review my mail? Let's start with the magazines. You can just throw the *Shiny Sheet* in the garbage. I've already read it."

Bernard tossed the newspaper into the wastebasket. As it came to rest, he saw Oliver's horrified face looking up at him. Perhaps this job would actually turn out to be amusing.

* * *

As the days passed, Bernard began to settle into a routine, spending afternoons with Oliver and evenings at Morningwood. His work at the club had been well received, with many members complimenting his accent. He had even been asked to fill in as maître d' and sommelier on a few occasions when other staff members had been too sick or too hung over to fulfill their responsibilities.

In contrast, working with Oliver had been a challenge. On his first day, Oliver had given Bernard a tour of the showroom, providing him with a description of each item, its list price, and the minimum price that he would accept for its purchase. Of course, the descriptions bore no relation to the truth because most of the pieces had been imported from Mexico City. Similarly, the list price was typically ten times the price that Oliver had paid for the item, and the price that he would accept was simply 20 percent below that inflated list price.

Oliver then explained his primitive methods for processing the payments for the few transactions that actually took place. Naturally, he was happy to accept cash, because he would then be able to avoid paying taxes, and he accepted checks because they were straightforward. He grudgingly accepted certain credit cards, despite the loss of a small percentage of income, but their use required that he call the credit card company to verify the card's status. Oliver's shop was perhaps the last in the Western Hemisphere that had not yet adopted the mechanical verification of credit cards. The remainder of his bookkeeping system simply involved the entry of the details of each transaction into a dusty, worn ledger.

Having completed this cursory course of training, Bernard usually found himself left alone in the shop. Perhaps it was a blessing to be free of Oliver's oppressive presence, but his days tended to be quite boring because customers were rare. On one such day, Bernard inspected a stack of Oliver's ledgers and determined that he had made an average of 50 transactions per year, or one transaction per week, during the preceding decade. Apparently, Oliver was able to pay his bills not because of the volume of his business but because of the exorbitant markups on his goods, although Bernard reflected that the daily receipt of past-due notices in the mail suggested otherwise.

Oliver wrestled with the twin demons of laziness and paranoia. He hated to work, but he could not overcome the fear that his clerks were stealing from him. Thus, in addition to the 30 minutes that he would spend in the shop each day reading his mail, he would also occasionally show up unannounced in an effort to catch the thieving crooks red-handed. Of course, he had never successfully done so, in part because there was nothing of any value to steal, but that simply convinced him that his clerks were far sneakier than even he had realized.

During these random appearances, Oliver would also take the opportunity to quiz the clerks on the details of their job to ensure that they were performing competently.

"Bernard," Oliver would begin, "I am a customer. Greet me and tell me about this piece of furniture."

"Alright. Good afternoon, sir, I see you are interested in this commode."

"No! You have to SELL, Bernard! You should have said, 'Sir, you have a very good eye. I see you are interested in this beautiful and important commode.'"

"You're right, Oliver, that is more persuasive."

"I have told you to call me Mr. Booth."

"Yes, I'm sorry, Mr. Booth."

"Now, how would you describe this statue?"

Bernard paused to think. "This impressive and important statue is a copy of a work by Michelangelo that is in the permanent collection of the Louvre in Paris."

"Do not say that it is a copy. They would probably figure that out, but you don't need to hit them over the head with it. And, by the way, you could also tell them that you are French and that you've seen the statue in the Louvre."

"But you told me not to mention that it's a copy."

"Enough of your back talk. Let's do some haggling."

"What's haggling?"

"Negotiating, imbecile. Try reading your English dictionary now and then. Suppose that I, as the customer, offered you $2,000 for the statue. What would you do?"

"I would agree to that price, because you told me to accept any offer over $1,500 for the statue."

Oliver looked distraught. "No, no, no! If they offer you $2,000, it means they're willing to pay $3,000! You have to think on your feet!" He paused and tried to calm himself. "Alright, that's enough for today. I will be out of the shop at some important client meetings throughout the rest of the afternoon." Bernard looked at him skeptically. "Please close up today and I will see you tomorrow at noon."

"Yes, Oliv . . . er, Mr. Booth."

"Dolt."

* * *

It was during one of those lonely afternoons spent reading *Hello* magazine that Bernard heard the "Marseillaise." Rather than stirring a feeling of national pride, the music caused Bernard to anticipate a lost tourist looking for directions to a more popular store, an elderly incontinent desperately seeking a bathroom, or a deliveryman dropping off some unsaleable item for Oliver's inventory. Instead, when he looked up he found Margaret Van Buren standing there looking irritated and slightly disheveled. She was holding the hand of a tall and tanned but clearly young blond boy who was dressed in the uniform of the Palm Beach Elementary School.

"Excuse me," she began, "I am so sorry to bother you, but my grandson is in desperate need of a bathroom and I was wondering if we might trouble you to use yours. I think this could be an emergency."

"I need to pee NOW!" the child bellowed.

"I would be happy to help you," replied Bernard, "but the only bathroom is in the shopkeeper's apartment upstairs and no one else is permitted to use it."

"I'm going to pee in my pants!" yelled the child.

"I understand," replied Bernard, "but perhaps there is a bathroom in the barbershop next door."

Bernard heard a rumbling from above and then the dull thud of Oliver's steps as he descended the stairs. He was wearing a tent-like silk kimono and looked a bit haggard.

"What is going on down here? What is all of this noise? I was just about to begin my morning ablutions!"

"Oh, Oliver," responded Bernard, "this young gentleman is in need of a restroom, but I was explaining that the only facility on the premises is in your private residence and that—"

"Call me Mr. Booth, goddamnit! Nobody is permitted to . . ."

As Oliver's gaze shifted from Bernard to the child to Mrs. Van Buren, a look of horror came across his face that rapidly metamorphosed into an expression of smarmy conciliation.

"Ah, Mrs. Van Buren, I did not immediately realize that you were the person accompanying this fine, strapping young lad. Of course he may use my bathroom. Bernard, show him upstairs. And Mrs. Van Buren, you yourself should certainly feel free to relieve yourself in my bathroom, if you are so inclined, as soon as your son is through."

"Martin is not my son, he is my grandson," she replied, "and my bodily functions are none of your concern. But thank you for your assistance. I will be waiting for him outside."

"Your grandson? No, you seem far too young to have a grandchild," said Oliver, rubbing his sweaty hands together anxiously.

"Please, spare me. I'm 73 years old."

"And you don't look a day over 39, if I may say so! Now, Mrs. Van Buren, please allow me to reintroduce myself. We met on New Year's Eve. My name is Oliver Booth and I am the patron of this shop. I was mistakenly seated at your table on that evening, and, unfortunately, the staff did not permit me to remain in your company."

Mrs. Van Buren inspected Oliver out of the corner of her eye. "Yes, I vaguely recall some commotion when we arrived at our table. That was you? How regrettable for you. Wait, didn't I see you in the newspaper?"

Oliver looked shocked. "Oh no, why would I be in the newspaper? I'm just a humble dealer of fine antiques. Please, allow me to show you around while you wait for your handsome young grandson to finish his business. You must be so proud."

"You don't seem to be in any condition to be at work, Mr. Booth. Your hair is a mess, you haven't shaved, you smell like a garlic field, and you seem to be wearing some kind of tent. To be honest, you look a bit deranged."

"Oh, Mrs. Van Buren," chuckled Oliver bashfully, "I had just awakened and I had not had any time to primp prior to your unexpected, but oh so welcome arrival."

"You just woke up? It's 1:30 in the afternoon."

"I have a condition that requires quite extended periods of rest."

"Now I remember!" interjected Mrs. Van Buren with excitement. "You WERE in the newspaper! I saw you on the front page! Weren't you that fellow who fell in the pool on New Year's Eve?"

"I didn't fall, some old idiot pushed me in. Perhaps I recall some mention of that debacle in the *Shiny Sheet*, now that you mention it."

"The *Shiny Sheet*? I doubt I saw your picture there. I left for New York early on New Year's Day. Oh, that's right, you were on the front page of *The New York Times*. I read it on the plane! Oh my, I remember now, how could I forget, you were absolutely soaked to the gills, and you were being held up by those brave young men who came to your rescue!"

Oliver was stunned. Not *The New York Times*! Most of his limited coterie of customers had apartments in Manhattan, and this kind of publicity was not going to help his business at all. He regrouped.

"Well, Mrs. Van Buren, let's just put the past behind us, shall we, and begin anew. Please allow Mr. Oliver Booth the pleasure of accompanying you on a brief tour of the history of fine French furniture." He extended his arm in the hope that she would accept his invitation, but his efforts were interrupted by a voice from upstairs.

"Mr. Booth?" called Bernard.

"Yes, Bernard, what is it? I'm very busy with a customer."

"I'm not a customer, I'm just waiting for my grandson," said Mrs. Van Buren.

"The lady's grandson seems to have an upset stomach," said Bernard. "Do you have any additional rolls of toilet paper?"

The child screamed out, "I need number two wipers!"

"Number two? I never agreed to that!" said Oliver. Remembering that the child was Mrs. Van Buren's grandson, he gathered himself and replied, "Bernard, I believe that there is one remaining roll of toilet paper in the bathroom closet."

"Mr. Booth, we will need more than one roll. The young gentleman has an impressive case of diarrhea, and he seems to have missed the toilet. In fact, completely."

"Oh my God, yuck," said Oliver.

Mrs. Van Buren was outraged. "Mr. Booth, the young boy is in distress. Go upstairs and help him. I'm sure he was confused by your facilities."

Clinging to the remote chance that he might make a sale, Oliver had no choice. He followed his nose up the stairs to offer his assistance.

* * *

Twenty minutes passed, and Bernard returned with the boy.

Mrs. Van Buren looked relieved. "Are you feeling better, my little prince?"

"Uh-huh."

"Did this nice young man help you with your little problem?"

"Uh-huh."

Turning to face Bernard, she asked, "And what is your name, young man?"

"Bernard Dauphin, madame."

"Well, *madame*! How continental! I don't recall having been called madame since I was in Paris last spring. It certainly has never happened in Palm Beach. You know, the word *madam* has quite a different connotation in this country!"

Bernard smiled. "So I have heard," he replied.

Mrs. Van Buren leaned forward and whispered to Bernard, "So, how did you get roped into working with this buffoon?"

"Well, Oliv . . . er, I mean to say Mr. Booth, suggested that my other job does not provide sufficient compensation, and he thought that I could be helpful in his shop. You know, because I'm French."

"Why would being French help you work in this shop? Isn't all of this furniture from Mexico?"

"Mr. Booth feels that these items are most persuasively presented to his clients as French antiques. He also feels that my French accent will help." Bernard paused and then continued in a lower voice. "Actually, just between us, I should mention that I selected one of these pieces myself. I accompanied Mr. Booth to an estate sale in Boca Raton a few days ago and I noticed it immediately. I could not convince him to bid on it, so I used my own money. He told me that I could try to sell it in his shop and that we would split any profits between us. He was actually quite insulting about the piece, but I had a good feeling about it. To be honest, though, I have very little experience in the field."

"Well, you just show me the piece that you selected, Bernard, and allow me to be the judge of its quality."

Bernard led her to the rear of the shop, where a commode stood in a dark corner of the back room.

"Is this the piece?" asked Mrs. Van Buren. "It's really difficult to see it back here. You know, you're not doing yourself any favors with this lighting. Could you bring it out into the center of the showroom, please?"

"Of course," said Bernard. He picked up the commode and negotiated his way to the center of the shop through a maze of gilded Mexican handicrafts.

Mrs. Van Buren walked around the piece, eyeing it intently. "This really is quite exquisite, Bernard. Well, I for one certainly think you have very good taste." She paused and smiled. "I'll tell you what, let's have a little fun with your boss. Tell me," she asked in a hushed voice, "what did you pay for this piece at the auction?"

"Quite a lot, for me at least. I paid $740."

"Bernard, you stole this piece. Wait, here he comes now."

Oliver gripped the handrail tightly as he descended the stairs. "Disgusting, absolutely disgusting," he muttered to himself. "I shall need to wash my hands with bleach." He reached the landing and looked up. "Ah, Mrs. Van Buren, I trust your grandson is feeling better. I'm so glad I could be helpful. Youthful tummies can become quite queasy with all of the sugar these children eat. Isn't that true, little boy?" Oliver reached out to tousle Martin's hair.

"Don't touch my hair, your hands were in the toilet."

"So adorable," said Oliver as he pinched the boy's cheek, perhaps slightly more vigorously than necessary, provoking a shriek of pain from the child. "Now, Bernard, I see you've taken the initiative to begin showing Mrs. Van Buren around the shop, but we should begin elsewhere, not with that beat-up old piece."

Mrs. Van Buren smirked. "But Mr. Booth, I spotted that piece myself as I wandered around your shop. I actually think it's quite nice. How much are you asking for it?"

Oliver looked surprised. "Really, well, wouldn't you prefer one of the pieces displayed in the window? They're much shinier. Can't you see how gold they are?"

"Yes," said Mrs. Van Buren disdainfully, "but it is in this piece that I'm interested. What is its price?"

"Let me check my ledger," said Oliver. He walked to his desk and began to leaf through his records, pretending to look for the listing of the piece and its price at auction. "Ah, here it is, Mrs. Van Buren. Because you are such an important member of our community and because I am hopeful that you will call on me for any future decorative needs you might have, I will not insult you by expecting you to haggle. I will simply give you my lowest price immediately, which is simply my cost to purchase the item, the fee that I paid to have it shipped to me from a chateau in France, and a modest commission. That price is $10,000."

Mrs. Van Buren remained expressionless. "I will pay you $2,000."

Oliver was unable to hide his dismay. "Oh, Mrs. Van Buren, I could never let this beautiful and important piece go for a price so far below my cost. Couldn't you see your way clear to pay just slightly more? I will try to remain open-minded, and I will offer you a compromise price of $6,000."

"I will pay you $2,000."

"Four thousand?" asked Oliver, hesitantly.

"Two thousand dollars," said Mrs. Van Buren, implacably.

Oliver gathered himself. "Alright! Two thousand dollars it is. But only on the condition that you return to my shop and consider additional purchases in the future."

"We shall see, Mr. Booth, we shall see. Now I will write you a check for $2,000, and I would very much appreciate it if you would both deliver this commode to my home at the end of the day. The address is 276 Via Bellaria."

Oliver disdained making deliveries himself, feeling that it was beneath him but also fearing that his morbid obesity and chronic hernia could lead to a catastrophic outcome. He knew that he would be able to convince Bernard to do all of the work in return for his share of the profits, however, and he would not miss the opportunity to inspect Mrs. Van Buren's home, which had been prominently featured in *Architectural Digest* three months previously.

Mrs. Van Buren handed her check to Bernard, who passed it along to Oliver. "Then I will see you both by 5:00 p.m. today?"

"Yes, Mrs. Van Buren, it will be our great pleasure," said Oliver. Bernard nodded in agreement. She and her grandson turned and left the shop.

"Well, Bernard, you got lucky with your little purchase. My compliments to you. You will receive your half of the profits as soon as this check clears. I expect that $500 should go a long way for someone with your limited means."

Bernard frowned. "My share of the profits is actually $630, Oliver, and you also owe me the $740 that I spent on the piece."

"Yes, yes, alright, and I've told you repeatedly to call me Mr. Booth. Now, I'm going to go back upstairs and sterilize myself. I feel like I have been soiled in every nook and cranny of my body."

* * *

Oliver's car was a Citroën from the 1950s. He thought that it conveyed an air of panache, despite the fact that it tended to emit flatulent brapping noises and puffs of smoke from its tailpipe at regular intervals, a problem that was exacerbated by Oliver's incompetent stewardship of the manual transmission.

Oliver turned onto South County Road. "Now, Bernard, do yourself a favor and do not expose your ignorance by attempting to speak," he said. "Simply carry the commode into the house, place it where requested, and return to the car. I anticipate that Mrs. Van Buren and I will have business to discuss, and your presence will not be needed. Have you ever fished?"

Bernard looked at him blankly.

"No? Well, neither have I. But I do know that once the hook is firmly seated in the fish's mouth, you can reel him . . . or her . . . in. And, Bernard, in the present case, the hook is your commode and the fish is Mrs. Van Buren. And a big fish she is too."

Oliver turned onto Via Bellaria and pulled the car into the driveway at number 276. Mrs. Van Buren's late husband had purchased the property in 1986, four years before his death, for slightly more than $2 million. Since then, Mrs. Van Buren had received a number of unsolicited offers from prospective buyers, the most recent of which had topped $30 million, but she had no interest in selling her beloved home.

The residence, known as Villa Ricchezza, had been designed in 1937 by Maurice Fatio, a gifted architect whose local reputation was surpassed only by that of Addison Mizner. The villa, which consisted of a 20,000-square-foot main house, a 10,000-square-foot guesthouse, and an additional

THE MISADVENTURES OF OLIVER BOOTH

5,000-square-foot building for staff, was built on three acres of land, an astonishingly large expanse for Palm Beach, where a typical lot size would be closer to half an acre or less. The grounds contained an Olympic-size swimming pool, two tennis courts, and an expansive, compulsively manicured lawn bounded by an intentionally wild and overgrown Provençal garden.

Oliver extracted himself from the car and told Bernard to untie the ropes securing the antique cabinet to the roof while he rang the doorbell. Or, more accurately, sounded the gong, which was activated with a tug on a velvet rope.

The door opened to reveal an elderly man in tails. "May I help you?"

"Ah, a manservant. Please tell your mistress that Mr. Booth has arrived."

"My mistress? Sir, my wife passed on three years ago, and I have never had a mistress."

"I mean, please tell Mrs. Van Buren that Mr. Booth has arrived."

The man looked at Oliver skeptically. "A Mr. Boot? She is expecting you?"

"Of course, my good man, I . . ." Oliver was startled to find that Bernard had already joined him in the entryway with the cabinet, which he had placed on a dolly.

The butler brightened. "Oh, I see, you are deliverymen! If you would return to your vehicle and drive around to the rear, I would be pleased to accept your goods at the service entrance."

"But—"

"James, who is there?" asked Mrs. Van Buren as she descended the sweeping grand staircase from her master bedroom.

"No one, ma'am, just a delivery. I have asked them to deliver their load in the rear."

"Oh, Bernard, and . . . you . . . what was your name? Please come in. That will be fine, James. Bernard, please bring the commode into the Great Hall. I have the perfect location for it."

Bernard rolled the cabinet through the doorway, followed by Oliver.

"Mrs. Van Buren, I'm sure you'll remember that my name is Oliver Booth, but I would certainly prefer that you call me Oliver. May I say that your home is magnificent? If I could just make a few suggestions, there are certain pieces that I have in mind that would make wonderful additions. For example—"

"Thank you for your concern, Mr. Booth, but my home is now complete. Bernard, please place the commode to the right of the far doorway."

Bernard rolled the piece to the only unadorned section of wall in the room and set it in place.

Mrs. Van Buren looked at the commode admiringly and said, "That looks beautiful, Bernard. Please, come and sit with me over here. I have some business that I would like to discuss with you."

"Bernard's presence will not be necessary, Mrs. Van Buren," interjected Oliver. "He is merely my part-time clerk, and I brought him along only because I am troubled by an abdominal weakness that does not permit me to lift heavy objects."

"Actually, Mr. Booth, I invited Bernard to sit with us because the business that I would like to discuss concerns both of you."

"Both of us?" asked Oliver, surprised.

"Yes, both of you. Please sit down."

Oliver and Bernard found their seats and looked on expectantly.

Mrs. Van Buren began. "Now, Mr. Booth, when I told you that my house is complete, I was, strictly speaking, telling you the truth. My guesthouse, on the other hand, which you may have seen as you entered my driveway, is essentially empty. As you may know, I have five children, each of whom has a bedroom in this main house, but four of them are starting families, and I would like them to have a little more space. So I must embark on a new project, which is to furnish my guesthouse in an appropriate manner. And I will need to complete this project quickly because those four children have coordinated their vacations in order that they might be able to stay with me next month. It will not be possible for me to interview other decorators and then choose a candidate who will be able to complete this project on time. That is where you come in."

Oliver was giddy with joy. "Oh, Mrs. Van Buren, I can't thank you enough for this opportunity! You will not regret your decision. I knew that if you could only see the beautiful and important pieces in my shop, you would recognize that we share the same sensibilities."

"Mr. Booth, at the risk of hurting your feelings, I will tell you that I want nothing to do with the goods in your shop. To put it bluntly, they are a bit equatorial for my taste. Instead, I would like you to act as my agents and purchase European antiques for me under my supervision."

Oliver looked confused. "Did you say agent or agents?"

"I said agents, Mr. Booth. You and Bernard will serve as my agents."

Oliver was aghast. "But why him? He's nobody. He's a waiter!"

"I thought he was your clerk."

"Well, he's also a waiter at Morningwood." Oliver looked at Bernard, his expression a mixture of scorn and triumph.

"Well, that's fine," replied Mrs. Van Buren as she smiled at Bernard. "I'm glad to see that you're trying to get ahead, young man. And next time I'm at the club, I will ask to have you as my waiter, and I will make sure that I leave you a nice big tip!"

"Thank you, Mrs. Van Buren," said Bernard, beaming.

Oliver glared at Bernard and persisted. "But my point is that he is not qualified to shop for antiques. He has no experience!"

"Actually, Mr. Booth, please recall that the only piece that I purchased from your shop was purchased for your inventory by Bernard, apparently against your objections."

"You told her about that?" Oliver asked Bernard, shocked. Bernard did not respond.

"Yes he did," said Mrs. Van Buren, "and to my mind, one of the most important gifts that a person can possess is an understanding of beauty. It is an intangible sensibility that should influence all aspects of one's life, and Bernard showed me that he has that gift. That's why it's quite important to me that he work with you as you embark on this project." Mrs. Van Buren realized that, as distasteful as it might be, Oliver might need a little stroking. "And I'm sure Bernard will gain a wealth of knowledge while working alongside you, Mr. Booth," she concluded.

"Yes, well, I'm sure that he will," replied Oliver huffily. "Now, Mrs. Van Buren, we will, of course, need to walk through your guesthouse, and we will need a set of floor plans. And then I would suggest that we drive over to Dixie Highway in West Palm Beach. There are some lovely antique shops there, and I'm sure that some of my friends will give you particularly attractive prices because of your association with me."

Mrs. Van Buren smiled. "Mr. Booth, window-shopping along Dixie Highway is a wonderful way to spend a rainy afternoon when one has nothing better to do, but aside from a few select shops, it is strictly for amateurs. You will not be purchasing furniture for me there."

Oliver looked puzzled. "Then where shall we shop?"

"I am sending you both to Paris," she responded. "Bernard, you can call in sick at the club. If they give you any trouble, please let me know. Now, have either of you heard of the *Marché aux Puces?*"

Oliver shook his head blankly. Bernard responded, "Well, that means flea market in French. Are you asking us to travel to Paris to shop for you in a flea market?"

"It's not really a flea market, Bernard. Well, some of the stalls on the outer edges might be a bit flea-ridden, but it's actually a densely concentrated group of antique stands where you'll be able to find everything that I'll need for my guesthouse. And, most likely, at very reasonable prices."

"But I don't speak French," said Oliver.

Bernard smiled. "I do," he said.

"Exactly!" said Mrs. Van Buren. "You see, Mr. Booth, Bernard's participation is already paying dividends!"

* * *

Oliver and Bernard were in the Citroën driving back to the shop.

"I'm not sure how it was that you engineered this little scheme, my friend, but I can promise you now that you will live to regret it," said Oliver. "I have spent most of my adult life in the study of fine antiques, and here you come walking into Mrs. Van Buren's home, a delivery boy no less, and you are offered a subsidized shopping trip to Paris! Ridiculous!"

"Mr. Booth, please think about our conversations with Mrs. Van Buren," replied Bernard. "You must realize that I did not say anything to her that might have led her to this decision. This trip is an exciting opportunity, but I had nothing to do with it."

"Oh really, my little French friend? And how did Mrs. Moneybags come to learn that you had been the one to select and purchase that commode? Hmm? Answer me that!"

Bernard hesitated. Oliver was correct that Bernard had taken the initiative to show Mrs. Van Buren the piece.

"So, you show her the commode and now you're this big antique expert who speaks French," Oliver snorted. "Well, I have some news for you, Bernard. You will accompany me to Paris, but I will make the decisions. Think of yourself as my valet."

Bernard rolled his eyes at Oliver, who was watching the road.

"As soon as we arrive back at the shop, we will plan and book our trip. I am not going to give Mrs. Van Buren any time to change her mind. We leave for Paris tomorrow."

PART II

PARIS

CHAPTER FOUR

O liver and Bernard were booked on Air France Flight 95, which was scheduled to leave from Miami International Airport at 5:05 p.m. and land at Charles de Gaulle Airport in Paris the following morning at 6:25. They had passed the one-hour ride from Palm Beach to Miami in silence, which was accentuated by the 15 feet of space between them in the back of the super-stretch limousine that Oliver had felt entitled to order.

Bernard had decided to forgo battling Oliver about the expense of the limousine because he had been successful in his efforts to book both of their seats for the flight to Paris in coach. Oliver had demanded that he be seated in first class, in part because he had never flown in first class, believing that he deserved an elevated level of service regardless of the dramatically higher price of the seat. It was not his money, after all, and he was traveling in the service of a very wealthy woman. Although Bernard had persuaded Oliver that there would be many opportunities for self-indulgence after they arrived in

Paris, Oliver had been stewing about his seat assignment ever since.

"I am not happy, not happy at all. I should not be required to fly steerage with my medical condition."

"What medical condition is that?" asked Bernard.

"That's none of your business. My physique simply prefers a wider seat. Come with me to customer service. I'm going to see if I can convince them to give me an upgrade."

Oliver and Bernard walked over to the Air France customer service booth, where a clerk looked up at them expectantly.

"*Bonjour*," said Oliver.

"Good afternoon, sir, how may I assist you?"

"I am booked on your flight number 95 later today and I was wondering if it might be possible to upgrade my seat."

"If I could just see your ticket, sir, I would be pleased to check for you," responded the clerk. She took Oliver's ticket and glanced at her computer screen. "According to your records, you are booked to fly with a Mr. Bernard Dauphin. May I see his ticket, please?"

"Oh, he doesn't matter, coach is fine for him."

The clerk frowned at Oliver. "No, I need to see his ticket because they were booked at the same time," she replied.

Oliver snatched the ticket from Bernard with a glare and handed it to the clerk.

"Alright, Mr. Booth, yes, a few seats are still available in first class. Would you like a one-way or a round-trip upgrade?"

"Oh, round-trip, please."

"That will be an additional $6,534, please. Which credit card will you be using?"

"$6,534? But I was hoping that the upgrade would be complimentary."

"But why would the upgrade be complimentary? I do not even see a record of your being a member of our frequent flier program."

"But I have a medical condition that requires a wider seat," said Oliver.

"A medical condition?" The clerk stood up and looked over her counter at Oliver's body. "Ah, you are obese!"

"No, I am certainly not obese!" Oliver paused to reflect. "Um, would it help if I'm obese?"

"Perhaps," said the clerk. "We usually require a doctor's note, but in this case your condition is obvious. Please give me just a moment."

Oliver did not know whether to laugh or cry, but it did appear that he would be receiving a complimentary round-trip upgrade to first class.

"Do you have any bags, sir?"

"Just this carry-on item, mademoiselle," said Oliver, refer-ring to his bulging, bright red wheeled suitcase which had been packed to the point of bursting, necessitating that a wide rubber strap be wrapped around its girth.

The clerk leaned over her counter to inspect the bag and recoiled with surprise. "Mr. Booth, that piece is far too large to be brought into the cabin," she said. "Please place it on the scale."

"Bernard, if you would be so kind?" said Oliver.

Bernard looked at him blankly.

"Bernard, my condition?" Oliver leaned toward Bernard and whispered more forcefully, "My hernia condition?"

Bernard shook his head in disbelief, but he took a deep breath, bent his knees, and hoisted the bag onto the scale, which promptly broke.

The clerk was approaching the limit of her patience. "Mr. Booth, if you cannot find a way to reduce the weight of that bag, I will be forced to charge you an additional fee and ship it to Paris on a cargo plane."

"No, that won't be necessary!" he exclaimed, panicking. "Let me see what I can do!"

Oliver leaned with all of his weight onto the bag and caused it to topple onto its side. He wrestled the rubber strap off it, and the locks sprung open from the pressure of its contents. Oliver lifted the lid and began to root around inside.

"Here, Mr. Booth, please allow me to help," said Bernard, less out of a spirit of generosity than a desire to see exactly what weighty things Oliver had deemed to be so important to the success of their trip.

"No, no! Private!" yelled Oliver, slapping at Bernard's hands. "Back off!"

But it was too late because Bernard had been able to look inside. Hesitantly, he asked, "Is that a corset?"

Oliver's eyes darted back and forth between Bernard and the clerk as he tried to come up with a reasonable explanation. "Perhaps," he said. "There are times that I require a bit of assistance confining my waistline."

Taking pity on Oliver, and wishing that he would leave, the clerk said, "Sir, please, don't worry. I'll accept your bag. Just make sure it's tightly sealed. We wouldn't want any of our luggage handlers to see your unmentionables, now would we?"

"No, I suppose not," replied Oliver, irritated but relieved.

"Here are your tickets, Mr. Booth." The clerk turned to Bernard and winked. "Mr. Dauphin, I have placed your tickets in a new folder to help you keep them in order. Now, I would suggest that you both proceed to Gate F16 immediately. Your flight will be boarding soon."

Oliver and Bernard stepped away from the desk. Oliver was beaming. "That, my young friend, is how it is done. A free upgrade to first class. I must say, I'm feeling quite magnanimous right now. From today forward, you may call me Oliver."

* * *

The preliminary boarding announcement was made, permitting first-class passengers to enter the plane. Oliver rose with a self-satisfied air and said, "I can already taste that first flute of champagne, my young friend. I wish you a good flight. I will see you in Paris. I hope you will be able to get some rest in steerage. I anticipate that I will feel refreshed and wish to begin our explorations immediately upon our arrival."

"Have a good flight, Oliver," said Bernard.

Oliver walked toward the Jetway holding a plastic bag filled with the celebrity magazines and candy he had bought at the newsstand. He offered his ticket to the gate agent, who inspected it and frowned at Oliver.

"Sir, we have not called your row yet. Please step to the side. It should be just a few minutes more."

Oliver smiled. "No, I'm sure I heard you invite all first-class passengers to board."

"Sir, I'm sure you must realize that you do not have a first-class seat. You are in 65-F. Since that seat is in the last row of the airplane, we will be boarding you first, but please step aside for just a moment."

"There must be some mistake," he said. "I was given a complimentary upgrade to first class. Now please look on your computer and reseat me in the appropriate section. This is outrageous."

Bernard noticed from a distance that Oliver seemed to have become involved in an argument, which was not uncommon in his interactions with service professionals. Perhaps he was angry because they were making him wait until he was seated to serve him his first glass of champagne.

Boarding of coach-class passengers began. Oliver was livid as he snatched his boarding pass back from the gate agent and entered the Jetway. Bernard moved forward and presented his ticket.

"Ah, you just made it, sir. Apparently you didn't hear our pre-boarding announcement. You are in seat 1-A. Have a nice flight."

"I'm sorry, which seat am I in?"

"1-A. Turn left as you enter the airplane. Your seat is in the first row."

Bernard was shocked. Clearly some mistake had been made, but he decided it would be best to simply proceed. He entered the plane, turned left into first class, and took his seat. Upon being offered a choice of champagne or orange juice, he selected a glass of champagne in Oliver's honor and settled back into his seat to review the dinner and breakfast menus. He was going to make the most of his time in first class, at least until he was caught. It didn't take long for a problem to arise.

"Excuse me, that man is in my seat! Please check his ticket!" Oliver was struggling to pass the flight attendant who, though slight and certainly approaching retirement age, had no trouble restraining him.

"Sir, calm yourself or you will be escorted off this airplane, regardless of your seat assignment. Please hand me your boarding pass and I will speak with the gentleman in the first row."

"Listen, that's no gentleman; he works for me, and if anyone should be in that seat, it's me!"

The flight attendant took the boarding pass and walked forward to speak with Bernard. "Sir, I'm so sorry to disturb you, but there is a man who is convinced that he should be in your seat, even though his boarding pass states that he is in seat 65-F."

Bernard handed the flight attendant his boarding pass. "I don't want to cause a problem," he said. "I would be happy to change seats with that man if it would be helpful."

She inspected his boarding pass. "Yes, seat 1-A, of course. Your offer is very kind, sir, but regrettably it is not permissible. With our heightened security, we are unable to allow passengers to sit in other than their assigned seats. Unfortunately for Mr. Brute, he will need to be content with seat 65-F. Again, I'm so sorry to have disturbed you, but I appreciate your patience. We must all work together to deal with these cases of air rage, you know."

She returned to Oliver. "Sir, that man is in his assigned seat, so I'm going to need to ask you to move to the back of the plane. We cannot close the aircraft door and push back until you are seated with your seatbelt fastened."

"Why, I can't believe he did this to me. He tricked me. I don't know how, but he tricked me."

"Sir, the young gentleman actually offered to trade seats with you, so his response was quite gracious, if you ask me.

Now, I would appreciate it if you would find your seat and fasten your seatbelt. And please try to move quickly, you have quite a distance to cover before you reach your row."

Bernard suppressed his desire to look back and watch the argument, knowing that if Oliver met his eye it would only cause an escalation of the difficulties. He reflected on the events of the last hour as the flight attendant returned to thank him again for his patience and freshen his glass of champagne. The Air France clerk that Oliver had badgered about an upgrade had seemed quite professional, but Bernard remembered her wink. Perhaps this was her revenge. It was lucky for Oliver that he wouldn't have fit in a pet carrier or she might have reserved a space for him in cargo.

* * *

As he approached the rear of the 747, Oliver discovered that seat 65-F was a middle seat in the middle section of the last row. On the aisle sat a heavyset woman in a sari whose meaty limb had already claimed the armrest for the duration of the flight. On the other side sat a toddler who was eyeing Oliver suspiciously. Next to the toddler sat his mother, who was casually flipping through the Air France in-flight magazine, and then his father, who had already begun working feverishly on his laptop computer. Thinking quickly, Oliver spoke to the woman on the aisle.

"Excuse me, ma'am, I'm sorry to bother you. It was intended that I would be sitting in first class, but I have been mistakenly assigned seat 65-F, which is right next to you. I wonder if it would be at all possible for me to exchange seats with you. I have a medical condition that requires that my legs remain extended if I must sit for long periods of time, and

I'm sure that as a woman you will be much more appealing to that delightful little child than myself." Oliver batted his eyes.

"No."

"Perhaps I didn't make myself clear—"

"No, I said. I, too, prefer to have legroom, and I need to be near the kitchen to prepare my dinner."

"Why do you need to be near the kitchen? You say you need to make your own dinner?"

"Yes, I prefer to eat food from my homeland rather than the Western food they serve on these planes. When we are in the air, I will be preparing my chicken curry. It is freeze-dried and I need only add hot water. There may be extra, and if you ask nicely, it is possible that I might offer you some."

Oliver was dismayed. Now resigned to his fate, he squeezed past the woman and collapsed into his seat. The toddler continued to eye Oliver as the scent of a befouled diaper spread through the air.

CHAPTER FIVE

Sitting in the taxi with Bernard as they traveled from the airport to their hotel in Paris, Oliver looked like he had just been through a food fight, with yellowish-brown deposits of curry trapped in the pleats of his pants.

"I will never forgive you for what you did to me on that airplane, Bernard. That was the longest ten hours of my life!"

"Oliver, I'm sorry. Remember, I did try to change seats with you but the stewardess wouldn't let me. And it isn't my fault that we had to sit on the runway for two hours because of snow. When does it ever *snow* in Miami?"

"Enough. Let us begin anew. At which hotel did my travel agent book our rooms?"

"We have a reservation at the Holiday Inn St.-Germain."

Oliver was horrified. "A Holiday Inn? In Paris? Why did you agree to a Holiday Inn? Couldn't you have selected a more elegant hotel?"

"I thought we should try to keep our expenses down. Remember, we're not paying for this trip. Your travel agent told me that the Holiday Inn is in a wonderful location and that one large room would be sufficient for our needs during our short trip."

"You booked only one room? I'm not sharing a room with you, boy! I will need to speak with the manager as soon as we arrive at the hotel. These arrangements are entirely unsatisfactory."

The taxi traveled through the gray outskirts of Paris, where building after nondescript building displayed advertisements for unfamiliar French industrial products. Entry into the perimeter of Paris brought a rapid improvement to the quality of the architecture, with the beauty and history of the city becoming more apparent with every passing block. Upon their arrival at the Holiday Inn in the bohemian St.-Germain-des-Prés quarter of Paris, a sleepy porter collected their bags as Oliver and Bernard proceeded through the front door of the hotel.

It was 9:15 in the morning, the hour at which most American travelers are dropped at the doorsteps of European hotels like so many exhausted babies, hoping desperately that their accommodations would be ready only to find that the departing guests had not yet vacated their rooms and would not do so for hours. Most of these unfortunate travelers are forced to wander the streets aimlessly, with intermittent stops to refuel with double espressos that become decreasingly potent as the effects of jet lag begin to sink in. This journey ends when they return to the registration desk of the hotel exhausted, disheveled, and halitotic, to be presented—in most but not all cases—with that most satisfying of rewards, a key to a room.

Oliver approached the desk and rang the bell despite the fact that a clerk was already standing there looking at him expectantly.

Anticipating that Oliver would be an American, the clerk responded in English. "Yes, monsieur, I am right here. How may I help you?"

"My good man, we are booked to stay in your hotel and I'm sure we could do much better, but I am exhausted and I would like to bathe, so we will simply check in and review our options later."

"Your name, monsieur?"

"Booth."

"Ah, yes, Mr. Booth. You and your young friend are scheduled to be with us for three nights." The clerk looked at Bernard lasciviously.

"We will see about that. Apparently, we have reserved one room, but that will clearly be insufficient for our needs. I must have my privacy as I perform my daily ablutions."

"Ah, yes, I see, two rooms would permit you to have your time together," said the clerk, again leering at Bernard, "and then your time apart to rest. That certainly makes sense, and I would be pleased to accommodate you, if only I could."

"But you can't?" inquired Oliver.

"Unfortunately for you, monsieur, our hotel—in fact, all of Paris—is fully booked due to the annual meeting of the Société des Fumeurs."

"The who?"

"The Société des Fumeurs."

"Who are they?"

"The Société is dedicated to the consumption and enjoyment of tobacco and tobacco-related products. I'm actually a member myself."

Oliver was confused. "What do people do, sit around and smoke? Why do you need an annual meeting for that?"

"Monsieur, in France we cherish our traditions, one of which is the God-given freedom to smoke whenever and wherever we please. Unfortunately, the fascist leaders of our country have changed the laws to take away that basic human right, but I can promise you, monsieur, that while they might extinguish our cigarettes, they will not extinguish our spirit!" The clerk's eyes began to glow with intensity.

The little energy that Oliver still retained was dwindling rapidly in the face of this burgeoning political debate. "Please, I promise you that I will not challenge your right to smoke if you simply provide us with our room. Is there such a thing as a nonsmoking room in this hotel? Although I enjoy smoking certain of the more stylish American cigarettes on occasion, the fumes from your Gauloises and Gitanes make me ill."

The clerk laughed. "Of course we have nonsmoking rooms, monsieur! They are very popular with our American clients. I must inform you that you will probably notice the aroma of smoke as you pass rooms inhabited by our French guests, but I can assure you that scientists in our country have found that it has no harmful effects. In fact, they have proven conclusively that inhaling cigarette smoke is actually beneficial because it exercises one's lungs."

"Fine, fine. We will take our one room and discuss our options in private."

"Wonderful, monsieur, your room should be ready at 3:00 p.m."

Oliver was distraught. "Our room isn't ready?"

"Oh no, monsieur. In fact, as I review the schedule of wake-up calls, it appears that the guest who will be checking out of your room will not even awaken for three more hours. Perhaps you would like to have a coffee in our café?"

"I'm not going to drink coffee for three hours!"

"Actually, your room will not be ready for six hours. The guest will not *awaken* for another three hours."

Pushed to his limit, Oliver said, "Where is your pay phone? I am going to call my travel agent. This simply will not do."

* * *

"Bernard, I have modified our reservations."

"You spoke with your travel agent?"

"Yes."

"But isn't it the middle of the night in Florida?"

"She is well compensated by her commissions to help me in my time of need. I told her to find me better accommodations and that money is no object. You may remain here because you seem to like this hostel."

"Did Mrs. Van Buren agree to that?"

"Unlike you, I am accustomed to a certain level of opulence, so I requested something befitting my position in the world. I may not be your Louis the Fourteenth, but I will surely do my best to be treated like him, particularly if someone else is paying. I will be staying at a chic and lively hotel on the Right Bank, near all of the most glamorous antique shops. The name of my hotel is the Roi du Luxe." Oliver rose to leave. "I will take a taxi to my new hotel and call you in an hour. I will then inform you of our shopping plans."

"That would be fine, Oliver."

"Enjoy your hotel," said Oliver, grinning, as he walked toward the door.

* * *

Oliver had not realized that a hotel called the King of Luxury would be unlikely to live up to its name. It was located in the ethnically diverse, somewhat seedy, and slightly dangerous neighborhood of St.-Ouen, coincidentally not far from the Marché aux Puces that would be their primary shopping destination. True, the hotel was technically located on the Right Bank, but it was outside the *périphérique*, the ring road that traces the boundary of the city of Paris, and an expedition to the fine antique shops near the Louvre would require miles of walking and a level of physical fitness that Oliver had never possessed.

Oliver had hoped to transfer to the King of Luxury as quickly as possible in order to have an opportunity to bathe and sup to his satisfaction. Unfortunately—and through no fault of his own—the specter of *les grèves* reared its ugly and unwelcome head. These intermittent and well-planned work stoppages are designed to protest what the French consider to be injustices against their natural rights. These injustices include any efforts to increase the workweek beyond 35 hours, to reduce the permitted number of vacation days to less than 29 each year, and to actually require the unemployed to make a reasonable effort to find gainful work before receiving their welfare payments.

As Oliver's taxi approached the Gare du Nord, its path was blocked by a barricade supporting a group of young Frenchmen who were waving flags, banners, and swords in an effort to remind passersby of the glories of the Revolution of 1789, the last great battle that the people of France might be said to have won. Oliver leaned forward to interrogate the taxi driver.

"Excuse *moi*, do you speak English?"

"A little, monsieur."

"What is going on here? Will this delay be lengthy?"

"These young people are fighting for their rights. They are very courageous."

"What are they protesting?"

"These students are protesting a reduction in the variety of cheeses that is available in their commissary."

"And?"

"That is all, monsieur. It is an outrage. When we support these youths, we are also supporting the French dairy industry. You would have us eating your American cheese, monsieur, in its little plastic sheets?"

"Certainly not. American cheese is, well, not just cheese that is American, but American cheese, you know what I mean? Anyway, is there another route we could take to my hotel?"

"No, monsieur. This taxi is not moving until *la grève* is finished. I stand shoulder to shoulder with my brothers."

"But I must get to my hotel. I am exhausted and I smell of curry."

"What exactly were you doing last night, monsieur?"

Oliver's anger was mounting. "I flew in from Miami on your Air France. At least *they* were not on strike!"

"They are today, monsieur."

"Enough. Tell me what I owe you for the pitiful distance we have covered and give me directions to my hotel. I will walk."

"As you wish, monsieur, but it is far."

"Nevertheless, Paris is a city for walking, I am told, and I shall walk."

* * *

Block after block Oliver walked, sometimes seeing the same landmarks twice, in the maze that is Paris, although most of his route looked more like an Arab souk. He had not planned ahead and he had no map to consult, so on those increasingly frequent occasions when his persistence and energy began to wane, he would attempt to ask passing Parisians for directions in his fragmented grade-school French. His mentioning of the name of his hotel was usually met with a vacant stare, in part because he tended to mistakenly proclaim that he himself was the king of luxury and not that he was seeking a hotel with that name. Those who were perceptive enough to understand that this smelly, exhausted American with his huge wheeled suitcase must be looking for a hotel did their best to assist him, but Oliver's hotel was not particularly well known, so it was primarily due to chance that he at last found himself standing at its entrance.

"Thank God, I have arrived," he said. The porter approached him and reached out to take his bag. Noticing the stains on Oliver's pants, he glanced at him quizzically.

"No, I wasn't at a party," responded Oliver defensively. "I was on *your* national airline, God help you. Now I'm going inside to check in."

Oliver entered the hotel and he was dismayed to find that its decor made him regret that he had ever left the Holiday Inn St.-Germain. To call the Roi du Luxe a hostel would be to offer it unmerited praise, but with his odiferous, disheveled appearance, he fit right in. He was desperate and he would raise no further objections.

"Yes, hello, kind sir, I am Oliver Booth. I believe my travel agent called you a little while ago to reserve a room for me."

"Yes, monsieur, I have your reservation here."

"Is the room ready?" Oliver asked hopefully.

"Certainly, monsieur. We actually have a number of empty rooms, and I can give you your key immediately."

"I thought that Paris was full due to the annual meeting of the Société des Fumeurs," said Oliver, puzzled.

The clerk burst into laughter. "Oh, monsieur, I'm sorry, but I believe someone was having a little joke with you. That is what we say to guests in hotels when they make unreasonable demands. 'I'm so sorry, blame the smokers.' Monsieur, there is no Société des Fumeurs, just hotel clerks who are unsympathetic. Now, if you will just let me make an imprint of your credit card, I will get you your key."

"Finally," thought Oliver, while fuming at the insult.

Handing Oliver an ancient skeleton key weighed down with an iron ball to prevent its theft, the clerk said, "Room number three, monsieur."

"Shall I take the elevator?" asked Oliver, gesturing toward the birdcage-like contraption.

"That won't be necessary, monsieur. Room number three is on this floor. If you walk past the bar and then turn to the right, go past *les toilettes* and then turn to the left, walk through the kitchen—you will see the loading dock on your right—and keep going straight, it's the first door on your left. You can't miss it."

"I'm not sure I caught all of that," stammered Oliver.

"Never mind, here is the porter with your luggage. Please follow him and he will show you the way."

Upon arriving at the hotel room, the porter placed the overloaded suitcase in the closet and turned to look at Oliver expectantly. Sensing no impending gratuity, he decided to provide an orientation to the room's limited facilities.

"Monsieur, as you will see, here we have the bed, there is the telephone, to my right is the *salle de bains*. You also have a television. Is there anything else I can do for you at this time?"

Oliver continued to look at him blankly.

The porter continued. "The window, built into your wall, may be raised and lowered. This door through which we just passed is your exit in the case of fire. It operates by turning this knob." The porter turned the doorknob in each direction. Still no response.

"Well, is there anything else I can do for you at this time, monsieur, or shall I leave you?" he repeated, extending his right hand.

Oliver, confusing the porter's expectation of a gratuity with a gesture of international friendship, reached out and shook his hand, saying, "Oh, I'm so sorry, it must be the jet lag, please allow me to thank you for showing me to my room. Now, if you'll excuse me, I'm sure you'll understand that I would like to freshen up."

The porter turned and left with a bewildered expression on his face. Finally alone, Oliver realized that his minimum requirements of a bathtub and a bed had been met, although not exceeded. He did not allow the remarkably shabby provisions of the King of Luxury to deter him as he stripped off his heavily soiled garments and threw them on the floor. Suddenly, and without warning, he was startled to hear the doorknob turn and see the door swing open. The porter was shocked to discover that Oliver was already stark naked.

"Oh, monsieur, I . . . I . . . am so sorry," he said as he began to giggle. "I neglected to leave you your key." His responsibilities fulfilled, the porter departed down the hallway, his laughs punctuated by loud snorts as he shouted, "Au revoir, monsieur, bonne journée!"

"In my current state of disarray, I certainly can't blame him for his reaction," thought Oliver. "I shall be much more presentable after I bathe."

And bathe he did, in rusty water captured in a stained porcelain tub that had been left untouched since the most recent German occupation. Oliver wrapped himself in a worn gray towel and sat down on the bed to think.

* * *

At 1:00 p.m. Paris time, after having waited four hours for his room to become available, Bernard decided that he should call Mrs. Van Buren to notify her of their safe arrival, as she had requested. Because her butler was outside the house supervising the gardeners, she answered the telephone herself after the second ring.

"Well, good morning, Bernard, or should I say good afternoon! How was your trip across the water?"

"It was very nice, Mrs. Van Buren, thank you. I was fortunate to be upgraded to first class at no additional charge."

"Really? How did you engineer that, you lucky boy?"

"I'm not sure. I think it had something to do with Mr. Booth's, I mean Oliver's, behavior at the check-in desk. He was quite demanding, and I think the clerk decided to punish him by upgrading me and seating him in the last row of the plane next to the kitchen."

Mrs. Van Buren laughed. "That sounds like our Mr. Booth, alright. Well, I'm glad that you had a pleasant flight. How is your hotel?"

"My hotel is fine, thank you. My room should be ready soon."

"You aren't in your room yet? I would have thought that you would have napped, bathed, and eaten by now. Isn't it lunchtime?"

"Yes, but check-in time is 3:00 p.m. and the hotel is full, so I've been waiting in the lobby."

"And how is Mr. Booth? Has he recovered from the shock of flying coach?"

"Well, to be honest, Mrs. Van Buren, he told me that this hotel is not up to his standards and he called his travel agent to find him a room elsewhere. He has moved to a hotel called the Roi du Luxe."

"The Roi du Luxe? With a name like that, it can only be a dump. Listen, Bernard, if your hotel is so bad that Mr. Booth canceled his reservation, why are you still there? I want both of you to be comfortable. Particularly you."

"This hotel will be fine, Mrs. Van Buren. Oliver just likes to be pampered. And I've been trying to save you money on our travel expenses."

"Nonsense, young man. You will leave that hotel this instant. Take a taxi to number 15, Place Vendôme, and ask for Julien. Tell him that Mrs. Van Buren told you to request her usual accommodations. Get yourself settled and then have Mr. Booth meet you there. Perhaps when he walks in the door he will learn himself a little bit of a lesson."

CHAPTER SIX

Oliver's jaw dropped as his taxi pulled up outside the Hotel Ritz. Spotting Bernard waiting just inside the porte cochère, Oliver jumped out of the taxi and hurried toward him, berating him all the while.

"This is absolutely unacceptable, young man. This is the finest hotel in the world. I don't know who you think you're going to fool, but when Mrs. Van Buren sees your hotel bill, you will most certainly be going to jail."

"Oliver, relax, I spoke with Mrs. Van Buren and it was her idea that I stay here. I told her that I would be perfectly happy to stay at the Holiday Inn, but she would not permit it. This will actually be less expensive for her because she maintains a room at the Ritz as her apartment. She's already paying for it, so she very generously suggested that I use it."

"I don't believe this. I'm staying at a dump and you're staying at the Ritz!" Oliver paused to think. "Wait, I have an idea, why don't we share the room? We would be able to shop much more efficiently if we are in close proximity to each other."

"I thought you told me that you didn't want to share a room with me?" replied Bernard with a frown.

"Oh no, my boy, you misunderstood me. I think it would be a wonderful idea. Why don't we just go inside and make the arrangements?"

Bernard's eyes narrowed as he considered Oliver's proposal. He really couldn't refuse the request because Oliver was his boss, and even if Oliver shared the room with him, as disgusting as that might sound, at least he would still be staying at the Ritz.

They passed through the revolving door and Bernard led Oliver over to the concierge's desk. Julien was on duty.

"*Ah, Monsieur Dauphin, votre chambre est-elle comfortable?*"

"*Oui, merci beaucoup, Julien, mais nous devrions parler anglais parce que mon collègue Américain a une question pour vous.*"

"Oh, monsieur, I apologize, but it was inconceivable to me that you were with Monsieur Dauphin," replied Julien. "How may I help you?"

"Ah, yes, thank you," said Oliver. "You see, I am in Paris with this fine young man to shop for antiques for Margaret Van Buren, who I have just learned is a valued client of yours."

"Oh yes, one of our most important and beloved clients."

"Yes, well, I'm sure it was just an oversight, but she would certainly prefer that Bernard and I share a room at your fine establishment to facilitate our shopping activities."

"Oh, monsieur, I'm sorry, but that would be quite impossible. I am under strict orders to permit only Monsieur Dauphin to occupy that room."

Oliver was becoming agitated. "But I'm sure that if you spoke with Mrs. Van Buren, she would tell you that she would be happy to have me join Bernard in her room."

"But you do not understand, monsieur, I *did* speak with Madame Van Buren just a little while ago, and it was she who gave me those strict orders, so there is really nothing that I can do for you."

Oliver brightened and said, "Perhaps you could find me a separate room and charge it to Mrs. Van Buren's account? As you know, I am here in her employ."

Julien frowned. "Monsieur, I have no authorization to provide you with a room at Madame Van Buren's expense, and I would not presume to call her with such a request." With a hint of a smile, he added, "And regrettably, monsieur, no other rooms would be available even if I had her authorization."

"No rooms at all? Not even the most expensive rooms?" asked Oliver.

"No, monsieur," responded Julien. "Perhaps you are familiar with our Société des Fumeurs. They are holding their annual meeting, and all of Paris—"

"Yes, yes, I know, the smokers, the smokers! Alright, I know when I'm not welcome. I suppose I'll just content myself with the King of Luxury."

Julien's eyebrows rose. "The Roi du Luxe, monsieur? In St.-Ouen? An interesting choice. Please permit me to advise you to keep your door locked at night, perhaps with a chair pushed up against it. They frequently have incidents in their bar in the evening."

"In the bar? My room is directly behind the bar!"

"Then it is even more regrettable that I have no accommodations to offer you, monsieur."

Bernard decided to take the initiative. "Oliver, let's have a cup of coffee and a croissant across the hall in the Vendôme Bar. We can plan the rest of our day."

"No," said Oliver forlornly, "I shall return to the King of Luxury and nap. You will meet me there at 7:00 p.m. and we will plan our activities over dinner at a restaurant in my neighborhood. I should not have to be the only one inconvenienced."

* * *

While Oliver napped, Bernard wandered the streets of Paris, avidly exploring his homeland's capital. He walked through the courtyard of the Louvre and the Jardin des Tuileries, down the Champs-Elysées to the Arc de Triomphe, across the Seine to the Eiffel Tower, along the riverbank to the Musée d'Orsay, and then back across the Seine to Notre Dame, where he boarded the Metro to St.-Ouen. He had wandered in and out of numerous antique shops and bookstores, and he had stopped twice for *café crème* and once for ice cream. All in all, it had been a wonderful afternoon, productive for having made an initial foray into the Left Bank's many antique shops and enjoyable for a variety of reasons, not the least of which was the absence of Oliver.

Bernard hoped that Oliver's much-needed rest had improved his mood. The desk clerk announced his arrival and Oliver appeared in the lobby just a few minutes later.

"I asked the clerk to recommend a restaurant in the neighborhood that has good authentic French cuisine," said Oliver. "It's the least we can do while we're in Paris. He made a reservation for us at La Maison des Cerveaux, which he said is just down the street on the left."

"La Maison des Cerveaux?" repeated Bernard. "That's a strange name for a restaurant. Did he describe the menu?"

"Tut-tut, my boy. Just keep your comments to yourself and perhaps I will be able to have an enjoyable meal."

La Maison des Cerveaux was what might best be described as a specialty establishment, as Oliver would soon discover. After a short walk, he and Bernard arrived at the restaurant, which was empty, and they were promptly seated.

"Oliver, I would be happy to translate the menu for you if it would be helpful."

"Nonsense, my boy, I am quite at home with French cuisine. Now, let me see what we have here."

Oliver perused the menu, trying not to act baffled. The waiter approached and asked if they were ready to order.

"Absolutely, my good man. I shall have the *cerveaux rôti*."

"Oliver, I don't think—"

"Bernard, what would you like to have for dinner?"

"But Oliver, I really don't think—"

"Bernard, please order. I'm famished."

"Alright. To be honest, I drank so much coffee and ate so much ice cream while I was walking that I still feel a bit full." He looked up at the waiter and said, "*Une salade mixte, s'il vous plaît.*"

Twenty minutes passed with forced conversation before the waiter returned with their food. An expression of horror was evident on Oliver's face as his plate was set down. On it he found layer upon layer of thinly sliced bumpy gray meat in a butter sauce and nothing else.

"Bernard, what is this?"

"I tried to warn you. You ordered roast brains."

"But I can't eat this, it's disgusting."

"Yes, I agree, but it's quite popular in certain provincial areas of France."

Oliver called the waiter over. "Look, *garçon*, I can't eat this, it's horrible. Take it away and give me back my menu. I will order something else."

"Oliver," said Bernard as his companion reopened his menu, "please allow me to translate for you. You don't seem to understand that half of the menu consists of dishes that contain brains. After all, the name of this restaurant in English is the House of Brains!"

"Do they have anything that doesn't involve brains?"

"Yes, of course. The left side of the menu has the heading '*Les Cerveaux.*' Avoid that side of the menu because all of those dishes contain brains. The right side of the menu has the heading '*Sans Cerveaux.*' There are no brains in any of the dishes on the right side of the menu."

"Thank God." Oliver studied the right side of the menu intently while Bernard excused himself to use the restroom. In placing his order, Oliver made a second terrible mistake, which both he and Bernard realized when the waiter returned with his plate of food. True, there were no brains on the plate, but Oliver had unwittingly ordered two huge bull testicles that had been fried and then served whole in a spicy peanut sauce.

"That's it, I concede," said Oliver. "Let's pay the check. I saw a McDonald's down the street and I doubt that they'll be serving any McBrains or McBalls!"

* * *

Upon returning to the Ritz after watching Oliver consume three Big Macs, two Croques McDo Chèvre, and three orders

of Les Frites, Bernard was handed a message from Mrs. Van
Buren asking him to call her at home at his earliest conven-
ience. She was hoping to speak with him before she left to
attend a benefit for the Society for the Differently Enabled,
which until the previous year had been called the Society for
the Physically Challenged. That was itself an improvement
upon the preceding name, the Society for the Handicapped,
and certainly upon the original name, the Society for Feeble
Cripples. The most recent name change had been necessitated
by the intensely politically correct atmosphere that surrounds
charitable fund-raising efforts during difficult economic times.

Bernard dialed the telephone number and waited. Mrs.
Van Buren answered the phone herself.

"Mrs. Van Buren, I received a message asking me to call
you," said Bernard. "I hope I'm not disturbing you."

"Not at all, Bernard. Thank you for returning my call so
promptly. It appears that there may be a problem."

Bernard was concerned. "What kind of problem, Mrs.
Van Buren?"

"Let me ask you a question, Bernard, and please answer
truthfully. Did you have a loud party in your hotel room this
afternoon, and did you invite a group of courtesans to join
you at that party?"

"Absolutely not, Mrs. Van Buren, I don't know where
you could have heard—"

"I know, Bernard, I know. I have already spoken with Julien, who checked with housekeeping and told me that your
room had been vacant during the hours of this supposed party. Now, a second question. Did you go to the hotel gift shop
and charge a bathrobe, a pair of slippers, and a gold pinky
ring to your room?"

"Mrs. Van Buren, I don't wear pinky rings, and I—"

"Don't worry, Bernard. I know it wasn't you. The salesgirl in the gift shop told Julien that an overweight American man who was perspiring heavily charged those items to your room."

"Oliver?"

"Yes, apparently."

"But where did you hear these things?"

"I received a call from your Mr. Booth a little while ago in which he presented me with the fabricated story of your wild party. He also told me that you had charged the items that I just mentioned to your room. It seems your friend is trying to set you up. Perhaps he feels you're cramping his style."

"Mrs. Van Buren, he's not my friend and he has no style to cramp. What do you think I should do?"

"Everything will be fine, Bernard. I have every faith in you, and I know that you will make this trip a success. But in the meantime, keep your eye on Mr. Booth, and try to have some fun. At *his* expense, for a change!"

* * *

Oliver met Bernard at the Ritz for breakfast at 9:00 a.m. the following day. "If I'm not able to stay here, at least I can dine here and charge it to your room, eh, my boy?" said Oliver, chortling.

"Yes, Oliver, that does seem to be a strategy that appeals to you."

"Now, what do you know about this flea market? It sounds quite shabby. Shouldn't we just concentrate our efforts on the Right Bank, where all of the finest antique stores can be found? Remember, the more expensive the goods, the higher my commission!"

"Oliver, Mrs. Van Buren specifically asked us to shop at the Marché aux Puces. She sent us to Paris for that purpose. If you would like to do anything else, I must ask you to call her to make sure that she is in agreement."

"No, no, no, I wouldn't think of disturbing her! Why don't we give this flea market a try? Tell me, what have you learned about it?"

"Well, while you were napping yesterday, I went on a long walk around the city and I stopped in a number of antique shops and bookstores. The antique dealers didn't really want to tell me anything. I guess they felt it would hurt their business. I found an excellent guide to the market at Shakespeare and Company, though, and I thought you would like it because it's written in English." Bernard offered the guide to Oliver.

"Have you read it yourself?" asked Oliver.

"Most of it."

"Well then, don't waste my time by making me read it too. Just give me a summary."

Bernard consulted his notes. "Alright, the Marché aux Puces, or flea market, is located in the north of Paris. Apparently it's in a bit of a seedy section, very Arab, called St.-Ouen." Bernard stopped short, suddenly realizing that the Roi du Luxe hotel was located in St.-Ouen, but Oliver didn't notice. Bernard continued, "The closest Metro stop is Porte de Clignancourt, so you should—"

"Forget that, I'm using a car service."

"Fine. The market is open on weekends from around 10:00 a.m. until late afternoon. It consists of a group of smaller markets called Biron, Serpette, Paul Bert, Vernaison, Malassis, and Dauphine. Each has a slightly different atmosphere, although you can find many different stalls selling antiques at every level of quality and price in each market."

"Fine. So there are many antiques dealers."

"More than a thousand, actually."

Oliver was impressed. "Really? That is quite a lot. So I wander in and out of these stalls. Let's say that I see something I like. What do I do?"

"Obviously, you ask for the price. Specifically, you state that you are an antiques dealer," said Bernard, smiling as he recalled the Mexican handicrafts that were on display in Oliver's shop, "and then you ask for the best price for export. After the dealer tells you his best price, you negotiate further. You then either agree on a price or you move on."

"What if we agree on a price? How do I pay? And what do I do with the goods? I can't be lugging armoires back to the hotel."

"The best option is to work with a shipping company. There are a few that have offices at the market. You give them your information and they give you a book of vouchers. When you agree on a price with a dealer, you fill out a voucher. You write down a description of the item and its price, the dealer's contact information, and your contact information. You then give one copy to the dealer, you keep one copy, and you give the last copy to the shipping company. After you've finished shopping and returned to Palm Beach, the shipping company will inform you of the total cost for all of the items. You then wire them the money for the goods and the cost of packing and shipping, which is usually around 20 percent of the total purchase price. They then go and pay the dealers, collect the items, and ship them to you."

Oliver looked pleased. "That is quite an ingenious system. It sounds simple."

"It is simple," said Bernard, "but the guide says that you need to be knowledgeable about the age and quality of the goods you are viewing and have a sense of what would be a fair price. The Marché aux Puces is so big that if you don't purchase an item because the price is too high, you will probably see something just like it again later in the day."

"Bernard, as I've already told you, I have no incentive to keep the prices down. The more I spend on an item, the higher my commission. Mrs. Van Buren is infinitely wealthy. She won't know the difference."

"Oliver, I think she actually knows a great deal about antiques. Remember, she's the one who told us to go to the flea market."

"Nonsense. I'm sure we'll have no problem with her. And I'm tired of your negativity. At least I'll be free of you while I'm shopping."

"What do you mean?"

"I'm going to the market alone, boy. Didn't you know that? What possible help could you be to me there?"

"Well, I do speak French."

"Yes, I know, that's why I'm going to ask you to write down on a sheet of paper the basic phrases that I will need to use as I shop. That should be sufficient for my purposes. I mean, I don't plan on discussing philosophy with these people, now do I? Although I'm sure those pseudo-intellectuals would love to have me try."

"Oliver, shopping really requires more than a few phrases."

"Bernard, as I'm sure you've already realized, I have a basic knowledge of French that is specific to my profession—'Antique French,' you might call it—so your little cheat sheet will only serve to help me through any rough spots that I might experience. Now get to work!"

Oliver handed Bernard a cocktail napkin and a stub of a pencil. "I am going to use the facilities. I will be bringing a newspaper with me, if you know what I mean. I expect that you will have completed your work by the time I return, which could be anywhere from 10 to 30 minutes from now." Oliver reflected on the gastrointestinal properties of food from McDonald's. It baffled him how it would sometimes cause him to feel slightly constipated, while at other times it would cause his bowels to liberate their contents all too readily.

Bernard was left alone. So Oliver had not only tried to set him up, he was also making no effort to conceal his desire to inflate his commission. Mrs. Van Buren had suggested that he have some fun with Oliver, but she had left him to his own devices in that regard. It seemed that Oliver had provided him with a perfect opportunity.

Bernard outlined two columns on the cocktail napkin. The column on the left would be a list of useful shopping phrases in English and the column on the right would be their equivalent in French. Or so Oliver would think. Instead, Bernard would introduce subtle, or perhaps not so subtle, mistakes into the translations that could end up causing Oliver no end of misery. Despite Oliver's earlier statement, Bernard knew that he had never studied French, a fact that had been confirmed the preceding night at La Maison des Cerveaux.

So, what phrases would a shopper need at the flea market? "Your products are beautiful." Bernard reflected and then, using the familiar form that the French would find so insulting, wrote, *"Tes fesses sont belles"* in the right column, meaning "Your buttocks are beautiful."

"Has this piece been refinished? Is it original?" became *"Est-ce que tu as eu la chirurgie esthétique? Ta poitrine est-elle vraie?,"* or "Have you had plastic surgery? Is your chest real?"

"What is the price of this piece?" became *"Combien demandes-toi pour passer une nuit avec moi?,"* or "How much would you charge for me to spend the night with you?"

Finally, "Do you know of another dealer who might have the item that I need?" became *"Connais-tu une autre salope qui pourrait me satisfaire?,"* or "Do you know of another prostitute who could satisfy me?"

Oliver would never get to the point of actually completing a transaction if he spoke the phrases as Bernard had written them. The dealers would take him to be at worst a lunatic and at best the American with the poorest command of French in the history of the Marché aux Puces.

Surely, Oliver was going to be in big trouble.

CHAPTER SEVEN

Oliver looked out of the window of the taxi goggle-eyed. All he saw were sidewalk stands displaying leather coats and sneakers, with no antiques in sight.

"*Monsieur, nous sommes arrivés aux Puces,*" said the driver.

"Where . . . are . . . antiques?" His infinitesimal knowledge of French had deserted him.

"*Quoi? Le prix est cinquante-cinq Euros, s'il vous plaît.*"

"What? Oh, the fare."

Although the Marché aux Puces was less than one mile from Oliver's hotel, the driver had taken a circuitous route around the perimeter of Paris. Oliver reached into his pocket for his wallet, oblivious to the deception. From it, he withdrew 50- and 5-Euro notes and handed them to the driver.

"*Merci,*" said Oliver. The driver scowled at the rotund American and drove off with tires screeching.

Oliver was totally disoriented. Wandering did not help. Instead, it simply caused him to become even more lost in this sleazy Algerian bazaar on the outskirts of Paris. As he began to fear for his safety, he spotted a sign for the Marché Serpette in the distance. Vaguely recalling from Bernard's tutorial that one of the markets went by that name, he turned and walked in that direction.

Oliver didn't know where to begin. The market was huge, with a different stall every ten feet, and most dealers were displaying items that would be appropriate for Mrs. Van Buren's guesthouse. Thirty minutes of exploration had passed when Oliver heard a commotion behind him. In one of the stalls stood a group of five men, one of whom was quite tall and clearly the leader. The tall man was speaking to the dealer, a young woman who appeared to be a bit anxious. Three of the flunkies who accompanied the tall man were cowering behind him, while the fourth held a demitasse of espresso aloft with trepidation. Remarkably, the trembling of the minion's hand did not cause the tiny cup to fall off the gleaming silver tray on which it was supported. The tall man was able to pick up the cup, bring it to his lips, taste the espresso, and then spit it out in an angry spray onto all four of his assistants, who simultaneously began to apologize.

"Too hot! Too hot!" he screamed at the underling holding the tray. "Are you trying to scald me? My coffee must be exactly 140 degrees Fahrenheit when it is presented! Didn't you check its temperature?"

The flunky looked as if he was going to be sick. "I'm so sorry, sir, but the café had only a French thermometer that measures temperature in centigrade. I had to check the temperature of your coffee in another way. A way that I now know is unreliable and entirely unacceptable."

"Another way? What other way?"

"Well . . . I put my finger in it."

"You what?!"

Oliver recognized the man. He was Kenneth Keen, interior designer to the stars, and he was known to be impossible. Never one to shy away from opportunities for professional advancement, and believing that he would be received as a peer, Oliver approached him and attempted to initiate a conversation.

"Oh, Kenneth! Oliver Booth. We met briefly when you were in Palm Beach for the International Fine Art and Antique Fair . . ."

Kenneth Keen exploded. "*Who* is speaking to me?! *Who* is speaking to me?!" He made an elaborate show of looking all around the stall while pointedly failing to look at Oliver. "Did I initiate a conversation with someone? *Who* is causing this disturbance?" His voice had taken on a progressively more screeching tone.

"Down here, Kenneth. As I was saying—"

"*Who* called me Kenneth? By whose leave is someone calling me Kenneth? First I am given an espresso that burns my lips, and now someone is calling me by my first name! Even my mother calls me Mr. Keen!"

"I'm sorry to have disturbed you, perhaps it would be better if I just . . ."

Keen glared at Oliver and said, "You! Little man, learn this and learn it well, you do not speak to Kenneth Keen. Ever. For any reason. You would not speak to me even if you saw that my coat was on fire. Well, maybe then you could speak to me, but at no other time! Now go! Good day!"

Oliver stepped back as the servants gathered around the designer. They began apologizing in unison for Oliver's behavior while casting withering glances at him.

Turning to the minion who was holding the silver tray, Keen said, "I don't know why I'm wasting time in this stall.

Rupert, you are my executive assistant, am I correct? Even though I may still choose to terminate you for your role in that debacle with the coffee?"

"Yes, sir," said Rupert with a trembling voice.

"Have you learned anything while you have worked under me during these last two weeks?"

"Oh yes, Mr. Keen, and I cannot thank you enough."

"Then why are we still in this stall?" Keen pointed at each of five statues of horsemen from the Ming Dynasty and began to comment on them in a calm voice. "This . . . and this . . . and this . . . and this . . . and this." He paused, smiled, and then screamed, "They're all too designed! They're too designed! They do not spring from the heart of the artist! As a Buddhist, I cannot bear artifacts that do not speak to my soul! These atrocities were clearly fabricated to bring to market!"

"Mr. Keen, they're 500 years old and the glaze is in beautiful condition," responded Rupert tentatively.

"Silence, fool. Enough. We leave. Now let us reflect on the needs of Mr. Rosenthal, the golfer, our newest client. Rupert, ask the salesgirl where I might find the LeRoy Neiman paintings."

"Yes, Mr. Keen."

Oliver looked on in horror and then exhaled deeply as Kenneth Keen and his entourage departed. He looked back at the dealer and they both smiled with a shared sense of relief. Trying to get back on track, Oliver decided that this would be as good a time as any to begin his shopping. Perhaps the dealer had been so exhausted by her encounter with the celebrated designer that she could be manipulated in their transaction.

"*Bonjour*, ma'am," he began.

The dealer smiled. "*Bonjour, monsieur. Est-ce que vous aimez quelque chose ici?*"

"Er, um," Oliver looked down at his cheat sheet. He decided to try to soften her up with a compliment. *"Tes fesses sont belles."*

The dealer looked at Oliver wide-eyed, but she responded with a tentative, *"Merci . . ."*

Oliver felt that this was an auspicious beginning. He gestured to a table and said, *"Est-ce que tu as eu la chirurgie esthétique? Ta poitrine est-elle vraie?"*

"Monsieur, je pense que vous . . ."

Oliver sensed that her initial confusion was giving way to rising irritation and proceeded more rapidly. "It doesn't matter if it's been refinished," he said out loud, and then continued to consult Bernard's notes. *"Combien demandes-toi pour passer une nuit avec moi?"*

The dealer was shocked. Her face bright red, she roughly ushered Oliver out of her stand yelling, *"Casse-toi, cochon!"*

Oliver then made his most unfortunate mistake. He read her the final question on his sheet.

"Connais-tu une autre salope qui pourrait me satisfaire?"

Oliver awoke ten minutes later on the floor of the woman's stall. He touched his hand to his sore head and it came away with a coating of blood. He found himself surrounded by a group of people that included two French policemen and two paramedics, all of whom were looking at him and grinning. The dealer stood above him with a triumphant expression.

Oliver was unsure as to how he had ended up in this painful and embarrassing predicament. He recalled the incident with Kenneth Keen and then bargaining with the dealer about a table. With effort, he retrieved a hazy image of the woman holding an andiron in the air and bringing it down on his head.

"These French can be so prickly," thought Oliver as he lapsed back into unconsciousness.

* * *

"She just went off on me for no reason! I don't understand! I couldn't have been speaking with her for more than a minute when she hit me on the head with that andiron. And for some reason my groin is feeling incredibly sensitive."

"Oliver, I read in the newspaper that when the police came, they found the woman kicking you repeatedly in your . . . male parts . . . and they had to pull her off you."

"The newspaper? This incident was in the newspaper? Not again! At least it was in a French newspaper this time and nobody back home will see it. How mortifying."

Oliver was lying in his bed at the King of Luxury nursing his wounds on the morning after the incident. A turban of gauze was wrapped around his head, and his legs were spread to speed the recovery of his most delicate region.

"Bernard, I am in no condition to shop, but shop I will. I will not have Mrs. Van Buren saying that Oliver Booth is unreliable. And I will not miss out on the financial windfall that this expedition should bring."

"What are you planning, Oliver?"

"Today we will return to the market. You will accompany me and serve as my translator. I will make all of the purchasing decisions. Due to my condition, I will require the use of a wheelchair, which you will push. You will also carry an umbrella to shield me from the rays of the sun."

"The rays of the sun? It's January and it's freezing outside."

"Nevertheless, I must protect my complexion."

"Oliver, I don't think it will be possible for you to return to the market today. The newspaper article said that you've been banned until you complete a psychiatric evaluation."

"What! Nobody told me that."

"And I really don't think you would feel particularly welcome if you did return. That dealer might have killed you if the police had not arrived."

Oliver reflected. "I suppose you're right. Perhaps this is our opportunity to explore the shops of the Right Bank."

"I'm sure that I don't need to remind you that it was not Mrs. Van Buren's intention for us to shop on the Right Bank, and it was not an accident that you were banned from the flea market," responded Bernard. "You brought it on yourself."

"How did I bring it on myself?" asked Oliver with annoyance. "First, I have to deal with that lunatic Kenneth Keen, and then that dealer hits me over the head with an andiron. I hadn't even begun my shopping when I was attacked and then banned from the market! How was it my fault?"

"Oliver, I'm not saying it was entirely your fault, but anyone reading that newspaper article would probably blame you. I mean, the things the dealer reported that you said to her, they were foul. Asking her if her chest was real, and wondering if she could give you the name of a prostitute? What were you thinking?"

"I wasn't thinking anything! I was just reading the sentences you wrote down for me!"

"Oliver, I thought you said you had a background in French. You must know that even the slightest change in the pronunciation of a word can change its meaning profoundly. The word *baiser,* for example—"

"Apparently so," said Oliver, interrupting Bernard. "Well, I won't be trying *that* again. Perhaps the best approach would be for you to go to the market on your own. I will give you an explicit list of the items that are needed and the minimum prices that I am willing to pay. If you follow my instructions to the letter, we might still end up a moderate success. Now get me a pen and some paper and leave me in peace while I prepare your marching orders."

* * *

During his short walk from the King of Luxury to the flea market, Bernard reviewed Oliver's notes, handwritten with a fountain pen in florid script, as well as the shopping list that they had prepared during their tour of Mrs. Van Buren's guesthouse. Oliver's notes were singularly unhelpful and, in fact, flew in the face of all of Bernard's better instincts. They contained injunctions to look for fancy, ornate furniture, preferably gilded, and to accept the first price the dealer asked in order to maximize Oliver's commission.

Bernard wadded up the sheets of paper and jammed them deep into the pocket of his jeans.

Despite Oliver's somewhat delicate disposition, his initial reaction to the flea market had not been unusual. Bernard, too, was shocked to find booth after booth selling sneakers, leather jackets, T-shirts, candies and roasted nuts, and phone cards. He knew from his guidebook, however, that these stands were merely an outer boundary for the market and that he simply needed to pass through them without being hit by a car or robbed to find himself in the antique section.

Bernard had a limited knowledge of antiques and their pricing, but because he had been educated in France, he certainly understood the periods within which the pieces of furniture had been made. His greatest strength, however, lay in his innate appreciation of craftsmanship and beauty, as Mrs. Van Buren had recognized. Bernard decided to target skillfully crafted pieces in fine condition from the 19th century, during the reign of Napoleon the Third, as he progressed through the market. In that way, he knew that Mrs. Van Buren would be satisfied with the quality of the goods as well as their more moderate prices. Oliver, on the other hand, would not be pleased.

Bernard chose to begin his shopping with the same dealer that had beaten Oliver senseless on the preceding day. She had become a bit of a heroine to him for having taught Oliver a lesson, although he did not entirely approve of the method she had used. Setting aside any slight feeling of guilt about his role in the matter, Bernard conjured up an image of Oliver ensconced in his bed at the King of Luxury with an ice pack on his nether regions and smiled.

Bernard approached the dealer warily, unsure if she might still be seething with anger.

"*Bonjour, madame, je voudrais voir—*"

"Coming through! Coming through! Step to the side, Mr. Kenneth Keen is coming through!"

Bernard turned to find Kenneth Keen, encircled by his phalanx of flunkies, walking rapidly down the aisle, jostling dealers and customers alike and leaving chipped and toppled pieces of furniture in his wake. The designer was wearing a flowing silken kimono that accentuated his towering but skeletal frame, as well as his trademark sunglasses, which enabled him to avoid meeting the gaze of those whom he considered to be beneath him.

Bernard observed that the lead servant was swatting passersby with a rolled-up copy of *Paris Match* to clear the path for Kenneth Keen, while others looked on in horror. Bernard froze as the group came to a halt directly in front of him, not realizing that he was blocking the aisle and impeding their progress. In an instant, the servant raised *Paris Match* high in the air and brought it down swiftly on top of Bernard's head.

"Ouch!" cried Bernard.

"Move for Kenneth Keen," demanded the underling.

"*What* is the holdup?" screeched the designer, his gaze cast heavenward. "I ask you, *what* is the holdup?"

"I'm so sorry, Mr. Keen," said the underling, glaring at Bernard, "but a foolish person is standing in our path and staring. Perhaps he is retarded." Bernard glared back at him as he stepped to the side, rubbing his head. "I taught him a swift lesson and he has moved."

Kenneth Keen was annoyed. "Listen, you fool, people do not stare because they are retarded. They stare because I am a celebrity. Perhaps someday you will do something notable and people will stare at you, although I highly doubt it. Now move! I must be back at my hotel in two hours for my seaweed wrap."

The group marched off, the lead servant continuing to wave *Paris Match* threateningly at anyone who dared to cross their path.

Bernard had an inspiration. He would follow Keen and his group, who would proceed to irritate all of the dealers and then pay inflated prices. Bernard anticipated that the dealers would consider any other customer to be an improvement upon Keen—particularly if that customer spoke French—and therefore would be more willing to accept lower prices on their goods after the windfalls that they would have just received at Keen's hands.

Bernard's strategy was a success. At the end of the day, he had accumulated a stack of 34 invoices listing a total of 102 items. Pulling out his calculator, he determined that the total cost to purchase those items would be 214,450 Euros, with perhaps another 40,000 Euros for shipping. Bernard guessed that if he had shopped on the Left Bank, those items would have cost twice that amount, while he didn't even dare contemplate the price that the usurers on the Right Bank might have charged.

As Bernard left the market, his feet were stinging from the miles he had covered, but he had a feeling of real satisfaction that he had done his job well, and honorably.

* * *

Bernard returned to the King of Luxury to review his purchases with Oliver and found him in exactly the same position in which he had left him.

Oliver likened himself to Marcel Proust, who had lived for many years as a neurasthenic recluse secluded in a cork-lined room. Oliver had learned about the author while reading the wrapper on a package of madeleines, the cookies that had had such a powerful hold on Proust's memories of his childhood. Oliver, too, had become a recluse, but thus far his period of seclusion had lasted only one day, and instead of working on a novel, he had simply watched music videos.

"So, Bernard, you tell me that your trip was a success. I will be the judge of that. Hand over those invoices." Oliver leafed through them, shaking his head and saying, "No, no, no, tsk, tsk, I could have done so much better. Bernard, have you learned nothing from me? Why are these prices so low?"

"I felt obligated to save Mrs. Van Buren as much money as possible. She's paying for our trip, you know."

"Oh, and I am eternally grateful to her to be sitting here, with my head cracked open and my groin throbbing, watching puerile music videos. I should have stayed in Palm Beach. Now let me look at some of these invoices more carefully." Oliver pulled out a thin blue sheet of paper and began to inspect it.

"Here, for example, a Napoleon the Third nightstand. Who knew that there were three Napoleons anyway? Couldn't you find anything from someone named Louis? And why did you waste your time buying nightstands? There's no money to be made on them."

"Because they were on our list and everybody needs a nightstand. And Napoleon the Third ruled France during a very important period. He—"

"I don't care. I simply do not care. Next. You paid 900 Euros for a daybed. 900 Euros? Why didn't you at least offer the dealer 1,000 Euros? Mrs. Van Buren would never have noticed. Bernard, it's as if you have no understanding of the antique business at all."

"Oliver, I have to say that I think I did very well. I purchased 102 items, probably three-quarters of everything we will need to decorate Mrs. Van Buren's guesthouse."

"*We* are not decorating her guesthouse. *I* am decorating her guesthouse. And you are going to go back to the market tomorrow and have the dealers tear up all of these invoices. We will not be purchasing these items."

"Oliver, that's wrong, and it's also impossible. These invoices are binding contracts. The deals are done. Sorry."

"Goddamnit, Bernard, you are ruining this trip. It has been a disaster. Alright, listen young man, tomorrow morning, whether I can walk or not, we are going to shop on the Right Bank and we are going to spend some money. You will not stand in my way. In fact, you will push me in and out of every shop while I do my work. It will not be easy, but I will find a way to make up for your stupidity."

"I don't think so, Oliver. Your court-ordered psychiatric evaluation is scheduled for tomorrow morning."

"It is?"

"That's what it said in the newspaper."

"It did? Well, then, you will meet me on the Right Bank as soon as this ridiculous evaluation has been completed. The psychiatrist assigned to my case will have no choice but to certify my mental health, don't you agree?"

"Yes, Oliver, I certainly agree that you are certifiable."

"Good."

* * *

Bernard called Mrs. Van Buren after he returned to the Ritz to give her an update on the trip.

"Oh, Bernard, it's wonderful to hear your voice. How are you getting along?"

"I'm doing very well, Mrs. Van Buren, thank you. I had a very successful day at the flea market."

"Did you go alone? Where was Mr. Booth?"

"He spent the day in his hotel room watching music videos."

"Really? That's not a very productive way to spend one's time, now is it, Bernard? I'm not paying for his trip so he can sit around and watch music videos. And isn't he a little bit old for that?"

"Well, to be honest, Mrs. Van Buren, there was a bit of a problem yesterday. Oliver has been banned from the market. At least until he passes a psychiatric evaluation."

Mrs. Van Buren laughed. "Oh, Bernard, I really shouldn't be stringing you along like this. I know all about yesterday's incident. It's been in a number of newspapers, including to-day's *Shiny Sheet*. They made the connection between the altercation in the market and Mr. Booth's little spill in the pool on New Year's Eve. You should have seen the cartoon on the editorial page."

"Oliver will not be pleased."

"Well then, we won't tell him. I'm sure he'll find out about it in due course. We wouldn't want him to get so discouraged that he would fly home early, now would we?"

"Why not?"

"Now let's just try to stick to our plan, Bernard," laughed Mrs. Van Buren. "Tell me about your day at the market. I trust you were more successful alone than you would have been if Mr. Booth had accompanied you?"

"Absolutely! I found 102 items for your guesthouse and the prices were all quite reasonable."

"Fantastic, Bernard. I knew when I saw the piece you had acquired for Mr. Booth's shop that you had a special talent for this kind of work. I look forward to hearing all about your purchases after you return. Tell me, now that your work is done, what are you going to do with your remaining time in Paris?"

"To be honest, Mrs. Van Buren, Oliver is planning to shop on the Right Bank tomorrow. He feels that the items I selected are too inexpensive and that he won't be making enough of a commission on them."

"Really, now isn't that interesting. He seems to be forgetting that I never discussed any form of compensation with him in the first place, let alone a commission. One would think that my subsidizing such a wonderful trip would be a sufficient reward. Bernard, please make sure that you accompany him tomorrow. I would prefer that he *not* buy anything unless you agree it's lovely and the price is fair. Alright?"

"I'll do my best, Mrs. Van Buren."

"It shouldn't be very challenging to manage Mr. Booth, Bernard. He's not very bright."

"I know, but he's quite emotional, and he can be very demanding."

"Just conclude your trip successfully and then leave the rest to me. People like your Mr. Booth need to be taught a lesson. I have a little something up my sleeve for him."

CHAPTER EIGHT

The following morning, Oliver's taxi pulled up in front of the building of the court-appointed psychiatrist. It was massive and old, probably from the early 19th century, and at the center of its facade were two huge wooden doors. Oliver stepped up to the intercom and pushed the button next to the doctor's name. After a few seconds, he heard a voice.

"This is Professor Doctor August Fick. Who is there, please?"

"Oliver Booth, Doctor Fick. I was sent by the . . ." Oliver glanced around nervously and whispered, "by the court."

"I prefer to be addressed as Professor Doctor Fick."

"I'm sorry Professor Doctor Fick. Could you buzz me in, please? It's very cold out here and I would like to get started."

"The modern world is in such a hurry. Rush, rush, rush. Tell me why you are in such a hurry, Mr. Booth."

"I would just like you to buzz me in so we can get started. It's very cold out here."

"But Mr. Booth, we HAVE started. From the very first sound of your voice, I have been developing a conceptualization of your psyche."

"Doctor Fick, please, I would be happy to talk with you in great detail about all of this, but I would prefer to do so in private. Where it's warm."

A pause. "I prefer to be called Professor Doctor Fick."

"Yes, yes, I'm sorry, Professor Doctor Fick, now please!" Oliver pleaded.

Another, longer pause was followed by an audible sigh of resignation. "Alright. Enter. You will find me on the fifth floor." The buzzer sounded.

Oliver pushed open one of the huge wooden doors and passed through. Noticing the absence of an elevator, he began to climb the stone staircase. Given that each floor was 15 feet high and that Oliver was not in peak physical condition, he arrived at Professor Doctor Fick's landing out of breath and perspiring heavily, a condition that was quite familiar to him. Professor Doctor Fick was waiting for him.

"Professor . . . Doctor . . . Fick," puffed Oliver, holding out his right hand, "it's a . . . pleasure . . . to meet you."

"Interesting, you mention pleasure and then you seek physical contact with me. Are you a degenerate? It would not surprise me, after the statements you made to that unfortunate young woman at the market." Professor Doctor Fick, a very short, hatchet-faced man, spoke with a screeching yet condescending tone.

"Doctor Fick, I can assure you—"

"I prefer to be called Professor Doctor Fick."

Oliver rolled his eyes. "Yes, yes, I'm sorry."

"Why do you roll your eyes like that? Are you having a seizure?"

"Certainly not. I just—"

"You are angry with me, thus you are angry with your father."

"No, I'm not angry at anyone, I just—"

"Good day."

Oliver was startled. "Excuse me, Professor Doctor Fick?"

"Good day. We are finished."

"But I just arrived!"

"As I said. Our work is complete."

"But . . . I was here for only a few minutes. What will you tell the court?"

"That is confidential. I am not at liberty to tell you."

"But I'm the patient! It can't be confidential for me!"

"Good day."

Oliver stood, in shock, and then proceeded to slowly leave the office, his head hanging low. "This is terrible," he thought, "simply terrible. The doctor, the professor doctor, is going to say awful things about me."

Disheartened and having lost all interest in shopping for antiques on the Right Bank, Oliver trudged away from the building. Rain had begun to fall since his arrival just a few minutes earlier. Oliver had neglected to bring an umbrella, and he soon became drenched as he walked toward busier streets, seeking a taxi. He would not find one, of course. They were on strike.

* * *

Oliver's hearing took place the following morning at 9:00 in the Magistrate's Court. He had been charged with simple assault, sexual battery, and petty vandalism, and a determination that he was guilty on all of those counts could lead to a sentence of as many as five years in prison. Remarkably, Oliver was also accused of "fostering an existential vacuum," an esoteric charge that was considered a crime only in France. Although that charge would not increase the length of Oliver's sentence, a conviction would require that he spend the duration of his imprisonment in solitary confinement to encourage him to reflect on the human condition.

The purpose of Oliver's hearing was to determine whether there were sufficient grounds to justify a full trial. An attorney had been appointed by the court, but he had been unable to meet with Oliver due to a previously scheduled game of *pétanque* with the prosecutor. Having already heard that his new client was an American antiques dealer, the defense attorney expected that the charges brought against him would most certainly be correct and that there would be no point in delaying the proceedings in order to find friendly witnesses. Although the attorney anticipated that the hearing would be a formality, the prosecution would call certain parties to place evidence supporting the need for a trial on record.

Oliver sat next to his attorney in the courtroom. At the appointed hour, the presiding magistrate entered the room. In a tradition unchanged since the Revolution, he wore not only a gown but also a powdered wig, as did Oliver's attorney and the prosecutor. Certain formalities were conducted in French, but the court shifted to English as a courtesy to Oliver as his case was called.

The presiding magistrate ordered the first witness to come forward. "Call Hélène Barbelé."

Oliver was confused. He didn't recognize the woman's name, but then out of the corner of his eye he saw her rise. Hélène Barbelé was the flea market dealer who had hit him over the head. Oliver unconsciously raised a hand to his forehead, which was still swathed in gauze. He felt his groin throb, but in pain rather than with pleasure.

The woman took the stand and was sworn in. The prosecutor began. "Madame Barbelé, thank you for being here today. The facts of this case are quite clear, and today's proceedings should not require a great deal of your time. Madame, please tell the court your occupation."

"I am an antiques dealer at the Marché aux Puces."

"Very good, madame, a noble trade, I'm sure. Now, if the defendant would please stand."

Oliver slowly rose to his feet, causing the pain in his head and groin to escalate.

"Madame Barbelé, do you recognize this man?"

"Of course."

"Please tell the court how you know him."

"He is the foul-mouthed lout who so rudely insulted me two days ago. And then he destroyed some of my property."

"Destroyed some of her property?" Oliver whispered to his attorney. "How could I have destroyed some of her property if I was unconscious?"

The prosecutor continued. "Madame Barbelé, please tell us how this man insulted you. How did he approach you? What did he say?"

"Well, he entered my stand at the Marché and he . . ." The woman paused, wringing her hands in a melodramatic fashion. "Oh, I cannot go on, it is far too demeaning!"

"Please, madame, the court understands how you must feel," said the prosecutor, glaring at Oliver. "This must have been a horrifying experience. Please try to continue. Your testimony may help us to protect the public from sexual predators in the future."

"Sexual predators?" Oliver asked his attorney, perplexed. "Are they referring to me?"

"Please, monsieur, these are very serious charges," he responded. "Your behavior disgusts even me, and I am your attorney."

"But I didn't do those things!" pleaded Oliver.

"Please, monsieur. I must ask you to remain silent."

The woman continued, casting a brief glance at Oliver. "That man complimented my body, and then he offered to pay me to sleep with him. When I objected, he asked me if I knew, as he said, 'another whore' who might satisfy his needs."

The spectators gasped in shock.

"Now, Madame Barbelé, am I correct in stating that you are not a prostitute?"

"No, of course not! How dare you!"

"No, no, madame, I'm sorry. I ask the question only for the record, a mere formality. I'm sure it's quite unlikely that you are a prostitute. Now, did the defendant provide you with any details regarding his desires?"

"No, but I'm sure that they are quite depraved." The woman looked over at Oliver and she was shocked to find that he was casually stroking his groin, not realizing that he was simply trying to relieve himself of the persistent pain that she had caused by striking that most delicate part of his male anatomy.

"You mentioned that the defendant destroyed some of your property. How did that happen?"

Oliver leaned forward in his chair, awaiting her answer.

"Well, after that man made his disgusting comments, I felt that I should defend my honor. I picked up a Louis the Fifteenth andiron and swung it at him, hitting him on the head. The andiron was dented by his skull and I will certainly no longer be able to sell it. It is a total loss. That andiron was worth 3,000 Euros!"

"Amazing, you dented the andiron on the man's skull. That must be quite a thick skull!" chuckled the prosecutor.

Oliver leaned over to his attorney, who was also laughing. "Can he say that, that I have a thick skull? That's a bit insulting. Shouldn't you object?"

His attorney leaned toward him and whispered, "Monsieur, if this woman dented her andiron by hitting you on the head, then you do have a thick skull. There is nothing to which I might object."

The prosecutor stated that he had no further questions for Madame Barbelé and she was dismissed. The magistrate ordered the next witness to come forward.

"Call Kenneth Keen."

Oliver was aghast. He would never be able to look Kenneth Keen in the eye again. Not that he had been able to do so in the first place.

"Monsieur Keen, the court would like to thank you for delaying your return to the United States in order to participate in this hearing."

Oliver slumped at the defendant's table with his face in his hands at the thought that Kenneth Keen had been inconvenienced for this mockery of a trial.

"I'm sure you realize that I am a very successful and busy, not to mention famous, person, sir," responded the designer, "but when I was informed of the way that this man had treated that unfortunate woman, I did not hesitate to make myself available."

"We appreciate your sentiments, monsieur. Of course, as you may recall, we did need to issue a court order and remove you from your flight at Charles de Gaulle Airport in order for you to participate today. That was quite a scene you caused in the Jetway. But, nevertheless, we appreciate your presence."

Kenneth Keen responded with a peevish look, but his arch expression soon returned. "Yes, well, perhaps I had not fully understood your request until you came to collect me. Please proceed."

"Monsieur Keen, do you recognize the defendant?"

"Yes, this distasteful person forced himself on me at the flea market two days ago, stating that we had met previously. Rest assured that I do not consort with people like this."

"What did this man say to you?"

"Nothing, really. I found his behavior to be so outrageous that I took my entourage and left immediately."

"Monsieur Keen, thank you for your comments. We now have corroboration of Madame Barbelé's account that the defendant was at the Marché aux Puces on the date in question and acting in an impulsive and disinhibited fashion."

Oliver leaned over and whispered, "Look, if you're not going to object, I may need to get a new lawyer. This proceeding is absurd."

The attorney was shocked. He responded in a loud voice that was audible to the court. "Monsieur, you must restrain yourself. Such inappropriate comments are not helping your already difficult case."

The prosecutor looked on smugly, anticipating that he would have no trouble obtaining a conviction.

The magistrate called the final witness. "Call Doctor August Fick."

August Fick scuttled rapidly from the back of the courtroom to the witness stand, cleared his throat, and with an ingratiating smile said, "I prefer to be called Professor Doctor Fick."

The prosecutor bowed and replied, "On behalf on the court, I apologize, Professor Doctor Fick. We are all certainly well aware of your reputation. For the record, though, could you briefly outline your credentials?"

"Of course, it would be my pleasure. I was born in Munich, Germany, in 1920. I attended Ludwig-Maximilians-Universität, but my education was interrupted by a call to serve in the military of my fatherland in 1941. While I was stationed in Lyon as an Oberleutnant with the Feigling Korps, I took advantage of your country's educational system to initiate my studies of the human mind. It was then that I developed a special interest in the most twisted of character disorders." Professor Doctor Fick cast a brief glance at Oliver and then continued.

"Following the conclusion of my military service in 1944 and a brief confinement by your government for purely administrative reasons, I returned to the fatherland to begin my training in psychoanalysis. I have since found some modest success treating patients with severe character disorders, criminal psychopaths and the like."

"And you have served as an expert witness in hearings such as the present one before?"

"Yes, hundreds of times."

"Very good, Doctor."

"Professor Doctor."

"Yes, Professor Doctor. Have you had occasion to interview the defendant?"

"Yes, I have."

"And what were your conclusions?"

"This patient is quite interesting. He is truly disturbed. He suffers from an Electra complex, which is unusual because that term typically refers to daughters who wish to destroy their mothers in order to marry their fathers. The patient perceived me, in my role as a male authority figure, to be the representation of his father, and, through certain actions that do not need to be discussed here due to proprieties, he made it clear that he was seeking to be physically intimate with me and thus marry me. Regarding the incident at the market, I have no doubt that he was acting out the rage that he feels toward his mother on that unfortunate woman, the antiques dealer who testified earlier."

Professor Doctor Fick looked over at the dealer and spoke to her directly, smiling. "Do not worry, my dear, he's really quite harmless. He would never act on his twisted desires." She nodded and smiled back at him. Oliver groaned.

The prosecutor asked his final question. "Professor Doctor Fick—"

"Thank you."

"—have you determined that there are any other factors that are relevant to this case?"

"Yes, the patient suffers from a seizure disorder that, when combined with his inherently disturbed personality, causes him to have difficulty controlling his explosive rage."

The prosecutor looked surprised, and then displeased. "A seizure disorder?"

"Yes."

"So you are saying that the defendant has a medical condition that contributed to his repulsive behavior?"

"Yes."

The prosecutor knew full well that the court would be hesitant to bring its full weight to bear on a person with a significant medical problem, and so he asked his next question with trepidation.

"Is this seizure disorder treatable?"

"Yes, certainly, there are many medications that could be used effectively."

"But is it correct to state that the defendant would continue to pose a menace to public safety even if his seizures were successfully treated?"

"No. He would continue to be a twisted, depraved individual, but he would be of no consequence to those around him."

The prosecutor was ashen. He realized that he should have contacted the professor doctor to discuss his testimony before the hearing, but after the game of pétanque there had been no time. This seizure disorder would be quite damaging.

The magistrate spoke. "I have heard enough. Would the defendant please rise?"

Oliver struggled to his feet.

"Oliver Booth, despite your disgusting, sickening comments to Madame Barbelé, the court has no choice but to find you not guilty of the charges due to your medical condition. All of the charges will be set aside pending two actions on your part. First, you must undergo a comprehensive evaluation for your seizure disorder and comply with any and all treatments that are recommended. Second, you are ordered to pay Madame Barbelé the sum of 3,000 Euros for the andiron that you damaged."

Oliver was shocked and spoke out impulsively. "But my liege, even if I did say those terrible things, SHE hit ME over the head! Look, I'm still wearing the bandages!"

The magistrate was not pleased. "So now you mock this court by admitting your guilt? You could have saved all of us a great deal of time if you had done so earlier. Monsieur Booth, I order you to pay Madame Barbelé the sum that she is owed before you will be permitted to leave this courtroom. And may God have mercy on your soul."

Oliver sighed and reached into his pocket for his wallet, which had become quite thin. He looked over at Madame Barbelé, who was glowering at him, and asked, "Do you take credit cards?"

* * *

Bernard met Oliver at the King of Luxury the following afternoon and they took a taxi to Charles de Gaulle Airport to catch their flight home. Despite Oliver's routinely horrid behavior during their stay, Bernard felt a bit sorry for him, in part because it was he and not Oliver who had been the source of the salacious comments that had resulted in so much trouble. As a sympathetic gesture, Bernard had taken the liberty of ensuring that they would be sitting together in coach on their return flight, given that there was no chance Oliver would be upgraded to join him in first class. It was the least he could do.

Oliver checked in his huge suitcase uneventfully, and he expressed some small appreciation to Bernard for changing his seat assignment as they walked toward the security checkpoint.

"Oliver, I'm sorry that you didn't have a better time on this trip. You know, we really did very well. I was able to buy almost everything we will need for Mrs. Van Buren's guesthouse, and that would not have been possible without you."

Oliver grunted. "I really would prefer not to discuss it right now, Bernard. I am absolutely shattered, and that seizure medicine they forced me to take is making me sleepy. Oh, I wish I were home right now with Napoleon. I know that my dog loves me, even if no one else does!"

A security officer nearby looked up at Oliver in surprise and said, "Monsieur, please repeat your last statement."

Oliver smiled and said, "Yes, I know, you French do love your dogs. That's one of your better qualities. I simply said that I was looking forward to returning home so I could be with my dog, Napoleon."

"Oh, but monsieur, you must realize that it is illegal in France to name your dog after the Emperor Napoleon. It is the ultimate gesture of disrespect. I will have no choice but to issue you a citation. You will need to pay a fine before you will be permitted to leave the country, and you must promise that you will assign a new name to your dog immediately upon your arrival in America."

"What?! That's outrageous! I can name my dog anything I like and nobody . . ."

Bernard grabbed Oliver by the arm and steered him away from the officer, saying firmly, "Listen, Oliver, after everything that has happened on this trip, don't you think it would be a good idea to do what the officer says? Remember, they almost put you in a mental hospital yesterday."

"They should put *him* in a mental hospital, that idiot." Oliver took a deep breath. "Yes, yes, I suppose you're right. As much as it galls me, I will comply with this man's demands."

Oliver turned back to the officer. "I'm sorry, sir, you are absolutely right. It was not my intention to insult your great emperor. I weep that a man of such stature—I mean his reputation, not his height—is no longer with us."

The officer looked at him skeptically. "Monsieur, please do not get carried away. The Emperor Napoleon died 200 years ago. I am simply enforcing the civil code."

Oliver walked with Bernard to the airport police station. He handed his citation to the officer on duty, who requested a photograph of the dog for the case file. Oliver fished around in his wallet and discovered a photo that had been taken of the two of them at the previous year's Independence Day celebration at the Gardens of the Society of the Four Arts. July in Palm Beach tends to be quite hot, and Oliver's bright red face and coating of perspiration made his discomfort readily apparent in the photograph. Napoleon's physiognomy was similarly poorly suited to deal with the intense heat, and he, too, looked miserable as he posed with his tongue hanging out, silently panting. The officer smiled as he looked at the photo and took it to the back office to show his commander. Oliver could hear laughter and a loud voice that shrieked, "*Regardez ce cochon-ci!*"

Oliver was annoyed. "What are they saying?" he asked.

Bernard attempted to remain noncommittal. "It's difficult to hear. They're behind that wall."

Oliver would not be dissuaded. "Oh, please, Bernard, they said '*Regardez ce cochon-ci!*' Now what does that mean?"

Bernard responded sheepishly, "It means 'Look at that pig.'"

"I hope they're not talking about my beloved dog. He may be a bit heavyset, but in no way does he look like a pig."

"No, I don't believe they're talking about your dog, Oliver."

"Good. I think."

Having spent the remainder of his funds compensating Madame Barbelé for the damaged andiron, Oliver was chagrined to discover that it would be necessary to ask Bernard to loan him the money to pay his fine. As Oliver handed over the cash, he muttered, "Anything to get out of this godforsaken country."

PART III

PALM BEACH

CHAPTER NINE

The flight home had been uneventful but tedious. The six-hour delay sitting on the runway due to another strike and the nine hours of in-flight monotony had been broken only by Oliver's sarcastic and mildly abusive comments about Bernard, the other passengers, and the coach-class video presentation, which included an episode from a long-ago canceled sitcom, a three-day-old summary of the news, and a presentation of the movie *Dirty Dancing*, which for some reason was available only in Cantonese. Bernard had resolved early in the course of their journey home that he would dispose of Oliver as soon as possible, and he had just done so, with Oliver stating as he exited the taxi at his shop that Bernard was useless, uninteresting, and without promise.

Although Oliver's sole intention upon his arrival home was to freshen up, Bernard had resolved to visit Mrs. Van Buren to review the trip with her before Oliver had a chance to present his list of inflated prices. Her estate was just a short ride from Oliver's shop, and Bernard had arrived before he had even had a chance to collect his thoughts. He paid the driver, requested a receipt, and stepped out of the taxi with his bag.

Palm Beach homes typically exist in a state of hushed serenity, and at times the island seems as if it might be uninhabited. Residents typically prefer to pursue their avocations in elaborately decorated, climate-controlled interior environments, that inclination defeating the purpose of residing in such a beautiful, unspoiled locale. Such was the state of Villa Ricchezza upon Bernard's arrival. He had not telephoned ahead, hoping to surprise Mrs. Van Buren, and when he sounded the entry gong, it went unanswered. He began to walk around to the rear of the house, standing on his toes and peering into every window that he passed. He observed a succession of opulent rooms, but no people.

As Bernard rounded the corner and turned toward the rear of the house, he heard a young voice yell, "Hey, aren't you that waiter?"

Bernard looked in the direction of the sound and realized that Mrs. Van Buren's grandson Martin was sitting by himself in her gazebo, looking over at him.

Martin continued to berate Bernard. "Are you allowed to be back here? This is private property, you know."

"I was hoping to speak with Mrs. Van . . . your grandmother," responded Bernard with mild irritation. "I've been doing some work for her in Paris and there are some important issues that we need to discuss."

Martin looked him over. "What, like whether she wants to have a cocktail with her dinner?" he said in a sarcastic tone. "Listen, I get to speak to her first. I've been waiting here since the school bus dropped me off."

"But it's only noon. Isn't it a little early to be dropped off by the school bus?"

"School ended early because the teachers had some kind of meeting. So, do you know where my grandmother is?" Martin's voice betrayed a hint of anxiety.

"No, I just landed a little while ago and I came directly here. I haven't spoken with your grandmother since I left Paris."

Martin looked concerned. "So what am I supposed to do?"

"Well, I'm sure she'll be back soon," said Bernard. "Please tell her that I stopped by to discuss some important business with her." He turned to leave.

"Oh no you don't," said Martin. "I'm a child and you're a grown-up, and if you leave me here all by myself, I'm going to tell the police. You're in charge of me now."

Bernard was aghast. "Oh no I'm not," he said. "I barely know you. How could I be responsible for you?"

"I'm going to start screaming, and you won't like what happens after that!"

"You can scream all you want, I—"

"POLICE! HELP! PO—"

"ALRIGHT!" yelled Bernard. "Alright. Calm down. I'll help you. Just don't call the police. Now, where do you think your grandmother might be?"

"I don't know," replied the boy in a singsong voice.

"What I mean is, can you tell me some places that she likes to go?"

"I don't know," Martin repeated in an identical tone.

"Now, really, you must have some idea."

"You can ask me all you want, but I still don't know," said the boy as he grinned at Bernard.

"So, you are now my responsibility but you are choosing to be totally unhelpful, is that the situation?"

The boy laughed but he didn't respond.

Bernard frowned. "Alright, well, one thing I know is that your grandmother is a member of the club where I work, so we will go there and see if anyone has heard from her. I'll need to check in at the club soon anyway if I'm going to keep my job. Pick up your backpack. We can walk there in just a few minutes."

"I'm tired. You carry it for me."

"Oh, please," said Bernard irritably, but he picked up the backpack and took the boy's hand for their short walk to the club.

* * *

After having spoken with Helmut König regarding his work schedule, Bernard entered the club employees' locker room and rapidly marched Martin to the rear, where he began to speak to him firmly. "Look, it's time for me to begin my afternoon shift and I can't have a young boy following me all over the club as I wait on tables. I'm going to give you some fun things to do, and I'm going to ask you to please be good and don't get me in trouble."

"Why should I?" asked the boy petulantly.

"Because I'm asking you nicely," said Bernard.

"Yeah, right."

"Alright, because I'm asking you nicely and I'm going to help you find your grandmother."

"Better, but keep going."

Bernard frowned and tried again. "Because I'm asking you nicely, and I'm going to help you find your grandmother, and I'm going to give you $20?"

"Even better, but what else?"

Bernard was annoyed. "Because I'm asking you nicely, and I'm going to help you find your grandmother, and I'm going to give you $20, and I'm going to strangle you and dump your body in the Everglades if you don't cooperate."

The boy looked scared. "Er, okay, it's a deal. What do you want me to do?"

Bernard thought for a moment. He needed to come up with an activity that would keep the boy occupied for a long period of time in a location where he wouldn't be noticed. Ideally, Martin would also take over one of his chores. Bernard had an idea.

* * *

After he had changed into his waiter's uniform, Bernard led the boy out of the locker room. They moved quickly through the basement, climbed a flight of stairs, passed through the kitchen, and entered a storage room where they found a large table stacked with tarnished silverware.

"Since I'm going to be paying you for your help, I would like you to do something that will actually be helpful," said Bernard. "The club uses hundreds of place settings of silver every night and it has been my responsibility to polish them before I begin my shift. Today it will be your responsibility."

"But I don't want to do that," said Martin. "The polish stinks. It will bother my asthma."

"Do you really have asthma?"

"Well, I have allergies."

"I've never heard of someone being allergic to silver polish, but I promise that I'll think of something else for you to do in a little while."

"I want my $20 now."

"If I give you the $20 now, then you won't do anything. Why don't I give you $10 now and the rest of the money at the end of the day?"

"Do you want me to start screaming?"

Bernard hastily reached into his pocket for his wallet. "Alright, alright, here's your money. Now get to work."

"What do I say if someone comes in and asks me what I'm doing?"

"That's a good question." Bernard thought for a moment. "Hmm, well, just make up something about being on a field trip from school, learning about how the club works and all that."

Bernard left to start his shift. After only a few minutes had passed, the maître d' entered the storage room to collect some clean silverware to begin setting the tables in the dining room. He was surprised to find Martin there.

"Who are you? What are you doing here?" he asked.

Martin didn't know how to respond. He remembered the things that Bernard had told him, but he had trouble getting the words out. "I, um, I'm on a field trip from my school."

"A field trip? Are you nuts? What kind of field trip?"

"To learn about how the club works."

"But why are you polishing the silverware?"

Martin was flustered. He had to think of something fast. "In my Social Studies class we're reading about the people of Central America. My teacher wanted me to polish the silverware to see what life is like for them when they move to our country."

The maître d' smiled. "Oh, I see, well that certainly makes sense. It sounds like you're attending a very progressive school. Personally, I don't know where we would be without the minorities. Ecuadorians are the backbone of the restaurant business, you know, and if it weren't for the Mexicans, there wouldn't be anyone to trim our plants. Listen, I need ten place settings right away; could you take care of that for me?"

"Sure, no problem," replied Martin with relief, wondering when Bernard was going to return.

* * *

Bernard had been ordered by Helmut König to serve cocktails at Morningwood's weekly self-help seminar, and he was hopeful that one of the many participants might have some information regarding the whereabouts of Mrs. Van Buren. Although he had worked at only one seminar previously, that experience had been sufficient for Bernard to recognize that the primary purpose of the gathering was to provide the sheltered wives of Palm Beach with the opportunity to trumpet the intellectual, emotional, and physical failings of their husbands. These self-help seminars were also one of the primary social events of the week at Morningwood, and the women who attended took the opportunity to be on display very seriously. Rings, bracelets, earrings, and watches fabricated from platinum and gold and encrusted with diamonds, rubies, and emeralds—all of these accessories served no practical purpose other than to signify the wealth of the husbands and thus serve as a source of reflected glory for the wives.

The leader of these seminars was Dudley Drane, whose sole qualification was a certificate in massage therapy, which he displayed prominently at the base of his lectern. The audience would have been satisfied with any certificate, be it in pet grooming, botany, or automotive repair, because any single qualification was one more than most of them had ever held.

Only one man was a regular attendee of these seminars. His name was Todd Flank, and the women whom he had dated referred to him as the Toxic Bachelor. He had been married while he was building his fortune in investment banking in New York, but soon after he had secured his financial future at age 39, he divorced his wife and moved to Palm Beach to enjoy an early retirement. He had been on the prowl ever since, and as word of his bad reputation had spread and the supply of unconquered women had dwindled, he had resorted to attending these seminars in a quest to find new blood. To the uninitiated, a few of whom could be found at each seminar, Todd Flank—with his extreme wealth, his ready wit, his trim physique, and his beautiful Italian wardrobe, not to mention his extreme wealth—was quite the catch.

Although it was a little early in the day for cocktails, not that the time of day ever really mattered for cocktails in Palm Beach, one or two or three drinks served to relax the women and cause them to be more active participants in the seminar, which often required a great deal of role-play. Dudley Drane spent very little time preparing for these seminars, knowing in advance that the cocktails would release the women's inhibitions and permit them to run the show for him. A few pithy comments and a selection of memorable aphorisms and he would be home free.

Drane opened the seminar. "Good morning, ladies and gentleman—"

"It's 12:45 in the afternoon, Dr. Drane, it's not the morning. We would never have cocktails before noon!" shouted one of the women, precipitating a round of titters.

Drane consulted his watch and agreed, and then he noted, "Please, ladies, even though I do hold a certificate of qualification in a healing art, I am not a doctor, but I do appreciate the esteem in which you clearly seem to hold me. Now, to begin. Today's topic is 'Difficult Men, Easy Women: The State of Marriage in Palm Beach.' Let me first ask if that topic brings out any feelings or thoughts in any of you."

"Difficult men? Difficult men? I'll tell you about difficult men," responded Justine Bentley with annoyance. Despite the investment of tens of thousands of dollars in cutting-edge dermatologic procedures and an outfit that consisted of tight lavender Capri pants and a midriff shirt that was straining at the seams to support her cantaloupic breast implants, Mrs. Bentley was clearly showing her age. "All my husband ever does is sit like a lump stinking up the house with his Cuban cigars," she continued, fuming.

"What would you like him to do?" asked Drane.

"I want him to go out now and then and socialize."

"Where would you like to go with him?"

"Please! *I* don't want to go out with him. The man is such a pill. I want *him* to go out and socialize and make some new friends."

"Wouldn't you feel threatened if he makes some new friends? What if he finds another woman?"

"Threatened? I HOPE he finds another woman! Or a man for that matter. That's not unheard of in Palm Beach, now is it?"

Drane was perplexed. "Well, I really couldn't say, but why on earth would you want him to find another woman?"

Mrs. Bentley rolled her eyes at the stupidity of the question. "Because then I could be rid of him, of course. Nothing would make me happier than to be free of his cigar smoke and his obnoxious personality forever!"

"But what about Rodrigo, your little Cuban friend, Justine? Doesn't he smoke cigars?" asked Prudence Pratt with a smirk.

"He can smoke anything he wants, my dear, as long as he stays in shape. And keeps my pool clean!"

Drane exhaled loudly. "Apparently, this topic is more complex than even I had understood. Why don't we move on to our next activity? As I'm sure you will all recall from our previous meetings, a little role-play can really help us get to the heart of these matters. Let's work with the issue that Mrs. Bentley just described, a perhaps unresponsive husband who smokes cigars in the house. Mrs. Bentley, if you would be so kind as to stand here next to me, I would be pleased if you would play the role of yourself. Now, we will need a man." Drane glanced around the room. "Ah, Mr. Flank, we can always count on you to be present. Would you be willing to help us today?"

"Of course!" responded Todd Flank as he stood up. "It would be my pleasure to help these fine women unravel the mysteries of the male psyche."

"Now, Mrs. Bentley," Drane continued, "I would like you to interact with Mr. Flank—"

"Please call me Todd. I prefer that everyone calls me Todd."

"Alright, I would like you to interact with Todd as you do with Mr. Bentley when he is smoking one of his cigars. How would you begin?"

Mrs. Bentley's face began to take on a reddish hue. "Gerald, you insensitive boor, how many times do I have to tell you to take your smelly cigars outside?"

"Now, Todd, if you can imagine yourself in Mr. Bentley's shoes, how do you think he would respond?"

"Well, I'm sure I would prefer to be in my own shoes; they're crocodile, you know," he said with a self-satisfied grin. Certain of the newer members of the audience giggled.

"Be that as it may, please respond to Mrs. Bentley's complaint. She just told you to take your cigar outside."

Flank reflected. "I would respond in this manner: 'Justine, I am so sorry that I hurt you with my insensitive behavior. Come into my arms, I want to feel you close to me, you precious jewel.'"

Mrs. Bentley beamed, triumphant. "Now that's more like it!"

Drane was not satisfied. "I'm not sure you understand the point of this exercise Mr. . . . um . . . Todd. I was hoping that you would play the role of Mr. Bentley, who Mrs. Bentley feels may be slightly unresponsive to her concerns."

"Slightly unresponsive?" interjected Mrs. Bentley. "What you mean to say is—"

"Yes, yes, I understand, Mrs. Bentley," Drane responded in a calming voice. "Todd, would you be able to try it again, with perhaps a bit more edge in your portrayal?"

"Not if it means that I have to be cruel, Dudley. I'm a lover, not a fighter, right, baby?" he responded, looking at Mrs. Bentley.

"How dare you call me 'baby'! Just because we had a little fling six months ago doesn't mean that you have the right—"

"Alright, alright!" said Drane. "I can see we're getting nowhere like this. Todd, if I could ask you to return to your

seat. Thank you for trying." He scanned the room and noticed Bernard standing toward the back, looking on in amaze-
ment.

"Excuse me, young man, could you step forward, please?"

Bernard looked to either side before realizing that Drane
was speaking to him. "Do you mean me?" he asked.

"Yes, please, you're the only remaining man present in the
room, and without you our role-playing experiment will be a
failure."

"But it would be inappropriate for me to participate in
this activity. I'm an employee of the club. I could get into a
great deal of trouble if I become too familiar with the members."

"Nonsense! Besides, if you *don't* step forward, I'll make
sure you get into a great deal of trouble anyway."

Bernard shrugged his shoulders, resigned to his fate, and
walked toward the front of the room.

"What is your name, young man?" asked Drane.

"Bernard Dauphin."

"And do I detect a slight accent?"

"Perhaps. I'm from France."

"Ah, you're French, perfect! You should have no trouble
portraying a callous, insensitive brute."

"Well, I don't think that's a fair—"

"Mrs. Bentley, please begin as you did before."

"With pleasure, Mr. Drane." She turned toward Bernard.
"Gerald, you insensitive boor, how many times do I have to
tell you to take your smelly cigars outside?"

Bernard thought carefully before responding and decided
that his best option would be to follow Dudley Drane's instructions implicitly.

"Because without me you would have nothing. I made all of the money, I bought the house, I bought the cigars, and I will smoke them wherever I like!"

Mrs. Bentley looked at Bernard in shock. She then slapped him so hard he saw stars, ending the seminar for the day. Bernard would need to pursue his inquiries regarding Mrs. Van Buren elsewhere.

CHAPTER TEN

Bernard returned to the storage room one hour later. By that time, Martin had finished polishing all of the silver, and he looked quite pleased with himself. "You know, you should be paying me more for all of the work I'm doing," he said.

"Twenty dollars an hour is very good pay for a ten-year-old," said Bernard. "Since there's nothing left for you to do here, I think it's time for you to move on to a different job, and you'll be happy to hear that you might actually receive some tips."

"What job?"

"I was just informed that they'll be starting the Doubles for Dermatitis tennis tournament in a few minutes, and they still need a few ball boys. The older members are unable to reach down to pick up the balls because of their hip problems, and the younger members will not reach down to pick up the balls because they feel it's beneath them."

"How come you're giving me another job? I'm just a kid, you know."

"I need to keep you busy just a little longer while I ask around about your grandmother. So far, nobody that I've spoken to has had any idea where she is."

"Do you really think I'll get tipped if I work as a ball boy?"

"Yes, you'll probably get some tips. Caddies get tips. Being a ball boy is like being a caddy. I haven't found the club members to be particularly generous, though. Now run on over to the pro shop. They'll probably have a uniform for you to wear."

* * *

The Doubles for Dermatitis tennis tournament had been founded following an epidemic of allergic reactions to cosmetics that had run through Palm Beach in 1993. It had been an annual event at the club ever since.

A loosely organized crowd of club members and tournament participants were slowly making their way over to Court One for the opening ceremony. Having changed into the required uniform of a white tennis shirt, white shorts, and white sneakers, Martin had been instructed to stand in a line at attention along with the other ball boys.

Jock Swensen had been the tennis pro at Morningwood for 23 years. Although he rarely gave lessons anymore, preferring to take a percentage of the fees of the itinerant young instructors who passed through town while he read months-old copies of *Tennis* magazine, he still displayed the leathery skin and wiry physique most often seen among seasoned tennis professionals, yachtsmen, and the homeless. He moved to the podium to begin the festivities.

"Gentlemen . . . and ladies . . . it is my great pleasure to welcome you to our annual Doubles for Dermatitis tennis tournament. Every year we meet up in this beautiful setting with one important goal: to raise money to fight a terrible disease. Dermatitis . . . and all cosmetics allergies." Jock lowered his head, wiped away a nonexistent tear, took a deep breath, and then looked up with a twinkle in his eye. "And play a little tennis!" The crowd let out a collective chuckle.

Jock continued. "As most of you know, our friend and club member Dick Richards and his celebrity partners have won this tournament for four years running, but this year he decided to give all of you a break. Oops, I guess that was a poor choice of words because he fractured his hip two days ago. Slipped at a cocktail party or some such thing. Since Dick is not here, the competition is wide open, and I wish you all luck. So, is everybody ready to play a little tennis?"

The crowd let out a halfhearted cheer.

"Then let's hit the courts!"

* * *

Although he had never before worked as a ball boy, Martin caught on quickly to his few responsibilities, the first and foremost of which was to stay the hell out of the way. He was assigned to a mixed doubles match, and he was surprised to learn that the team that would win had been predetermined based on the size of the players' donations to the Dermatitis Foundation. Thus, it was merely a formality for Jack Phlapp, at 87 years of age the oldest ambulatory club member and one of the wealthiest, and his partner, Mies Nainen, who had been the first Finnish lesbian to reach the quarterfinals at Wimbledon, to play against Lady Caroline Hardcourt and her partner in tennis and romance, the rugged Simian Pride, whose sole claim to tennis fame was his runner-up showing at the Bangladesh Open in 1983.

Although the outcome of the match was preordained, Jack Phlapp played as if it was not. Given his limited mobility, his strategy involved taking a position at the exact center of the court and barking out instructions to his partner, who was forced to sprint from side to side and from the net to the baseline on virtually every point. On rare occasions, a ball would be hit near Phlapp, but his reactions had been so dulled by the ravages of age that he was never able to raise his racquet in time to respond. Regardless of the hopeless efforts of Phlapp and his partner, however, Hardcourt and Pride made sure that most rallies ended in their opponents' favor.

Phlapp treated those around him, including the ball boys, as he had treated his adversaries in the boardroom—that is, badly—despite the ostensibly charitable goals of the tennis tournament. This was the sole reason why Martin was happy to see Bernard walk onto the court as the match concluded. He turned to leave with Bernard but stopped when he heard Phlapp shouting to him.

"You, boy. Stop there."

"Yes?" Martin became concerned that he had done something wrong.

"Isn't there something you're forgetting?"

Martin was confused. "Am I?" he asked.

Phlapp smiled. "You most certainly are, young man. Aren't you going to thank me?"

"Thank you?"

"That's better. You're welcome. I thought you might be able to show a little appreciation for the tennis lesson that I just gave you. And I would like to show you my appreciation for your own efforts."

Phlapp unzipped a pocket on the cover of his tennis racquet and reached in. "Here you are, young man, a shiny new quarter. Thank you for your hard work. Keep it up and you may just turn out to be like me when you're a grown-up." The old man turned and limped slowly away.

Martin walked over to Bernard. "You were right, I got a tip," he said.

"How much?"

"A quarter."

"It could have been worse. You could have received nothing."

Martin looked at Bernard skeptically.

"We need to get you into clean clothes," said Bernard. "I've found another job for you."

"Not another job! I need a break!"

"I know, Martin, but I need to keep asking around about your grandmother. It's like she vanished into thin air. Palm Beach is such a small town that I just can't understand how nobody has seen her."

"Alright, one more job, but that's it. And I'd better start making more money. A shiny new quarter isn't going to buy me anything!"

* * *

Bernard and Martin had returned to the employee locker room.

"Now, Martin, I'm going to need to leave the club for a little while," said Bernard. "I have to meet with a Mr. Booth regarding some personal business. Do you remember him? You used his bathroom when we first met?"

"What am I supposed to do while you're away? Remember, I'm just a child and you're responsible for me."

"You will do what I was supposed to be doing. You will work at the late afternoon tea service and stand next to the dessert table with the cookie tray. All you need to do is hold out the tray and people will take what they want. You can manage that, can't you?"

"I don't know. What if I dropped the tray and they found out that you weren't there to do your job? What if they found out that you forced a kid to give out cookies while you were somewhere else having fun?"

"Alright, what will I need to give you to make sure you *don't* drop the tray of cookies?"

"Twenty dollars."

"I already gave you $20."

"I meant another $20."

"Listen, Martin, I don't make a lot of money."

"Do I need to start yelling? Grandma told me all about you and how she's paying you to shop for furniture for her. I'm sure you have 20 more dollars you can give me."

"Alright, alright. I suppose I don't have a choice. Now come with me. I need to find you a uniform that will fit. There was a midget who worked here last season, but he was fired for drinking on the job. I think his uniform might still be hanging somewhere in the locker room."

* * *

Martin stood by the dessert table, cookie tray in hand, dressed in the former waiter's tiny uniform. Although he was dressed in standard waiter attire, he felt conspicuous because he was clearly too young to be holding a job. Further complications arose when Velma Sample, the supervisor of the wait staff, arrived.

Appropriately, given her family name, Miss Sample enjoyed partaking of the club's culinary concoctions, a practice, she suggested, that helped her keep the wait staff informed of the qualities of the items they were serving. She was therefore quite heavyset, and, regrettably, she tended to wear brightly colored caftans which—particularly on windy days—made her look like she was wearing a circus tent. While making her rounds, Miss Sample spotted Martin holding his tray of cookies and looking furtively out of the corner of his eye. Wondering why this young boy was dressed as a waiter, she approached him.

"Excuse me, young man, but who exactly are you?"

"Who, me?"

"The boy inside the waiter's uniform. We fired Rodolpho the midget at the end of last season, so you can't be him. What is your name?"

"Martin."

"Do you have a last name, Martin?"

"Van Buren."

"Your name is Martin Van Buren?"

"Yes."

"Do you take me for a fool? That's the name of a president, not a boy. What is your real name?"

"That *is* my real name, and I don't like it any more than you do."

"Alright, Master Martin Van Buren, how do you happen to be standing here holding a tray of cookies? Somehow I doubt that you're old enough to have your working papers."

Martin thought quickly. Although it wouldn't have caused him a great deal of distress to tell Miss Sample about Bernard skipping out on his work, he felt confident that the flow of $20 bills would continue unabated if he continued to play along. He decided to try to pull rank on her. "My grandmother told me to make myself at home at the club," he said. "She told me that I could do anything I wanted, and I wanted to play waiter."

"Well, your grandmother can tell you any little old thing she chooses, but that doesn't mean it's going to come true, especially on my watch. Now, where is your grandmother? I think I'm going to have a little talk with her."

"She's not here."

"Oh, that's awfully convenient for you, isn't it? Perhaps I'll just give her a call. What is your grandmother's name?"

"Margaret Van Buren."

The woman paused and then asked, "You don't mean THE Margaret Van Buren?"

"That's the one."

Velma Sample forced herself to brighten. "Well! That changes everything, doesn't it? I absolutely adore your grandmother, and anything that she says goes, as far as I'm concerned. Young Master Martin Van Buren, you look absolutely adorable in your little waiter's costume—"

"Uniform."

"Yes, uniform, exactly, and you just keep on handing out those cookies for as long as you like. And have a few yourself! But please don't mention our little conversation to your grandmother, okay? We'll keep it our little secret?"

"I don't know," replied Martin, "the things that you said, they . . . frightened me a little. I may have to talk to her about that."

"Oh no, young man, don't do that! What can I do to reassure you? Please, I'll do anything to make sure that you're having fun!" said Miss Sample anxiously.

Martin thought for a moment and said, "Whenever I'm not happy, grandma buys me a toy."

"Fine, fine, that's a wonderful idea!" she replied. "We don't have any toys around here, of course, but perhaps I could give you a few dollars and you could buy yourself a toy the next time you're at the store. How much do you think a little toy would cost?"

"Twenty dollars."

"Twenty dollars? That's an awful lot of money. I don't think—"

"I'm getting frightened again," Martin threatened.

"No, no, $20 would be just fine," she said as she reached into her pocket for her wallet. "Just please make sure that Mrs. Van Buren doesn't hear about this."

"Give me another $20 and I'll even say nice things about you," said Martin with a grin.

The woman frowned at Martin, thought for a moment, and handed him another $20 bill. "You're quite the little entrepreneur, aren't you? Well, enjoy handing out your cookies. I still don't know why you're here, but at this point, I don't want to know. Good-bye."

Velma Sample walked off, relieved to have extricated herself from the situation, as Martin shoved the two additional $20 bills into his pocket.

CHAPTER ELEVEN

Bernard entered Oliver's shop to find him relaxing in a large, carved, heavily lacquered wooden throne-like chair, wearing a red velvet bathrobe with white trim that caused him to look not unlike Santa Claus. Noticing Bernard, Oliver rolled his eyes and returned to reading the new issue of *Majesty* magazine that had arrived earlier in the day. He ignored Bernard as he approached.

"Hello, Oliver," said Bernard. "I thought I would stop by to go over our receipts. I'm sure Mrs. Van Buren will be quite eager to pay for her goods and have them shipped to Florida. As soon as I find her, that is."

Oliver frowned at Bernard and replied, "I'm sure that she will be eager to receive her goods, but I'm also sure that I won't be needing your assistance to make my presentation."

"She did say that we should work together, Oliver. And don't forget, I have all of the receipts, so you won't be able to do very much without me."

"Fine," Oliver grunted, "but I can assure you that I am looking forward to the day that you are once again out of my life and I will be able to serve Mrs. Van Buren in an independent capacity. I anticipate that my decorative efforts will yield a layout in *Architectural Digest* which will bring an onslaught of new clients and the success that I so richly deserve."

Bernard sat down on a turquoise garden stool and reached into a folder for the receipts. He pulled out a sheaf of papers and began leafing through them. "How would you like to do this, Oliver?" he asked.

"Alone," Oliver replied, "but apparently that's not an option. Instead, we will proceed in this manner. You will serve as my secretary. You will read me a description of each piece of furniture and then state the price that was agreed upon. I will then determine the appropriate price to be charged to Mrs. Van Buren. If we focus, we can be finished in 20 minutes. I have just begun running a warm bath and I will not let you ruin it for me."

"Oliver, what do you mean you will determine the appropriate price? The prices were already determined at the Marché aux Puces."

"Your naïveté makes me ill. *This* is what I mean. It is standard practice for decorators to charge a commission for the products that they purchase for their clients. That commission is compensation for their experience and hard work. Certainly you can't have a problem with that."

"What amount of commission did you have in mind?" asked Bernard.

"Well, let's think of it this way. If Mrs. Van Buren had bought all of the same items on Dixie Highway in West Palm Beach, their prices would have been three times what they were in Paris. Not that she would have been able to find everything she requires on Dixie Highway. Keeping in mind that she will still need to pay to have the items shipped to Florida, which should cost—"

"Twenty percent of the purchase price?" interjected Bernard helpfully.

"Yes, 20 percent of the purchase price," repeated Oliver irritably, "that would leave an incremental profit of . . . let's see, three times the purchase price minus the shipping . . . carry the four . . . no, wait, you divide . . . anyway, that would leave a very nice profit that goes directly into my pocket. Does that answer your question?"

"You're going to almost triple the price of these items? That's fraud, Oliver."

"No, it's simply good business. Now butt out of my good business and do as you're told. Begin reading me the list of items that we purchased."

Bernard glanced at the top invoice. "The first item is a Napoleon the Third commode, and the price is 2,000 Euros," he said.

Oliver smiled. "List that as a Louis the Fifteenth commode. The price will be $5,000. You see, Bernard, using my system, we don't need to waste time on conversion rates."

"But Oliver, first of all, the piece is not Louis the Fifteenth, and second of all, there is no way it's worth $5,000."

"Continue, boy."

"But Oliver, if this is the way you—"

"Continue, I said!"

"Alright, but please try to be reasonable. The next item is a Louis the Fifteenth . . . that should make you happy . . . *semanier*. The price is 3,500 Euros."

"What's a semanier?"

"What's a semanier? You're supposed to be an antiques dealer and you've never heard of a semanier? It's a tall cabinet with many small drawers." Bernard thought to himself that reproductions of semaniers must not be big business in Mexico.

"You can keep your sarcastic comments to yourself, Bernard. You will list that item as a Louis the Fourteenth semanier, and the price will be $8,250. Sometimes it looks better to avoid round numbers."

"Oh, I don't believe this, Oliver," said Bernard with frustration. "Your behavior is totally unethical. I will not be a party to this." As he cast his eyes downward in dismay, he noticed an unfamiliar invoice. "What's this? A 17th-century painting of Saint Gisella? Who is Saint Gisella? I didn't buy this. And it's listed as having been carried home. There must be some mistake."

Oliver snatched the paper from his hand. "Now Bernard, you just forget about that. I'm sure we don't need to concern ourselves with some inconsequential painting."

"Oliver, do you know something about this? The price is listed as 5,400 Euros. I haven't even seen this painting. I'm sure I could call the dealer and find out what happened."

"I know exactly what happened, Bernard. Upon my arrival at the so aptly named flea market, I made a single purchase. I bought that painting of Saint Gisella. If you French pagans studied your Bible more religiously, you would have known that Gisella is the patron saint of persons afflicted with eczema, although there have been reports that her divine intervention has also helped people who were suffering from psoriasis, boils, and athlete's foot. I was smart enough to ask for the painting to be delivered to me at the King of Luxury or it, too, could have suffered grievous damage in the attack brought down upon me by that psychopathic dealer."

"Oliver, why did you buy a painting of this Saint Gisella?"

"Well, Bernard, there's something particularly important about that painting, and if you had treated me with the respect I deserve, I might have told you about it."

"What is it, Oliver?"

"No."

"You can tell me the secret. I'm sure I would be interested."

"No. You were mean to me."

"I was just saying we shouldn't be charging these artificially high prices to—"

"See, you're doing it again! And you wanted me to tell you my secret."

"Then *don't* tell me your secret. I don't want to know."

"Alright, Bernard, the secret is . . ." Oliver looked around furtively to ensure that they were alone in the shop, even though it would have been reasonable for him to anticipate the absence of customers, and then said, "the painting weeps!"

"The painting weeps? What does that mean?"

"Saint Gisella! She weeps! The dealer told me that if I shine a light on the painting from just the right angle, then that's what I'll see!"

Bernard looked perplexed. "Saint Gisella really cries?"

"No, you idiot, it's a painting. She doesn't really cry. She just LOOKS like she's crying. I thought it would be appropriate for Mrs. Van Buren to purchase this painting for me as compensation for all of the difficulties that I endured in my efforts to shop for her. And I have a very strong feeling, my intellectually challenged little friend, that in addition to eczema, psoriasis, boils, and athlete's foot, Saint Gisella may also be the patron saint of unappreciated antiques dealers!"

* * *

Bernard returned to the club later that afternoon. He had been told that he would be required to work at a benefit that was being held that evening to raise funds for the Hammertoe Foundation. Bernard knew that Martin's skills would be insufficient in such a setting, given the demanding nature of the club members, and he regretted that Martin would miss that character-building experience, but he had another plan to keep the boy occupied that evening.

Bernard found Martin serving drinks to an elderly woman and a much younger man, and he held back to permit him to finish his work.

Martin placed the drinks on a small table in front of the members and said, "Here you go, a glass of Chardonnay for you, ma'am, and a gin and tonic for your son."

"I'm not her son, I'm her husband," said the man as he glared at Martin. "We've been married for three weeks now."

"I'm sorry," said Martin, "she just looks much older than you."

Now it was the woman's turn to glare at him as she replied, "Young man, haven't you been told that it's impolite to discuss a woman's age? The fact that I am married to such a vital young man is no business of yours. Men of a certain age marry young bimbos all the time and . . ."

Her much younger husband shifted uncomfortably in his seat.

"Darling, I didn't mean to imply that *you* are in any way a bimbo. Only women can be bimbos, of course. Speaking of age, aren't you a little young to be serving drinks in a bar?" the woman asked, turning toward Martin.

Martin looked at her nervously. He decided to try the response that had worked most effectively throughout the day. "My parents are European."

The elderly woman nodded in understanding. "Yes, I have heard that those Europeans are more progressive than we are, although I must say that children really shouldn't be serving liquor. But I suppose that's none of my business. Thank you for your help, Rodolpho."

"You're welcome," replied Martin through gritted teeth, irritated that he was being forced to wear the midget's name tag. He turned to walk away, only to run into Bernard.

"Hello, Martin. I see things are going well."

"Don't you mean Rodolpho?" asked Martin. "People have been calling me that all day. And where have you been? You're lucky I've been making money, otherwise I would have called the police and reported you for child abandonment."

"How much have you made?"

"That's none of your business."

"Don't worry, I'm not going to take your hard-earned money."

"I've made $212, and that doesn't include the tip from that old lady."

"I'm not sure she's going to be giving you much of a tip after your comment about her age."

"Maybe her husband will leave me a tip."

"Martin, I'm surprised you haven't learned by now. The only reason he married her is *because* of her money. His primary goal in life is to make sure that as much of it as possible goes into his pocket and not to some kid dressed up as a waiter."

"Well, then, you can leave me her tip."

"Listen, Martin, I have an even better reward for you. Have you ever dreamed of attending an incredibly fancy dinner party?"

"I've been to lots of those. My family is rich, you know."

Bernard rolled his eyes but ignored the bratty comment. He inspected Martin's uniform and then removed the name tag. With that simple act, the boy was now ready for his big night out.

* * *

Velma Sample was standing at the entrance to the ballroom in a well-worn cocktail dress. She looked bored, but she brightened as Bernard and Martin approached.

Bernard began. "Good evening, Miss Sample, this young man is—"

"Oh, I know who this fine young man is, Bernard, and he looks so handsome in his suit! How are you, Master Van Buren? Did you give away all of your cookies?"

Martin stared at her.

Bernard continued, fabricating a tale in order to ensure that Martin would be well taken care of throughout the evening. "Miss Sample, young Martin's grandmother, Mrs. Margaret Van Buren, had been intending to attend tonight's benefit, but she has been detained due to unforeseen circumstances. She telephoned to request that Martin be assigned the best available seat because she did not want her absence to ruin his evening."

Martin looked shocked. "Bernard, I don't want to—"

"Nonsense, young man, I'm sure Miss Sample will seat you with a very amusing group of people. We'll make sure you won't miss your grandma!" said Bernard in a childish, mocking voice.

"No, but I . . ." sputtered Martin.

Velma Sample took over. "Well, no seat has been purchased for Master Van Buren, Bernard, but given his grandmother's status at the club, I'm sure that I can look the other way. I hope she is well. What was it that detained her?"

Bernard thought quickly. "She said that, um, apparently her little dog was eaten by a very large lizard . . . that escaped from a pet store."

"Oh, how horrible! And disgusting! Well, Bernard, I will certainly do my best to make sure that Master Van Buren has a fine evening." She looked down at her list of reservations. "Now, where can I find an empty seat?"

Bernard interjected, "Miss Sample, I think I can be of some assistance. I have been assigned Tables 1 through 5 tonight. If you seat Martin at one of my tables, I'll be able to keep my eye on him."

"Tables 1 through 5? Bernard, you certainly have come up in the world!" she replied with a smile. "I would be happy to take you up on your thoughtful offer. Reverend Palsy had been scheduled to sit at Table 1, but I just received word that he will be unable to attend this evening's festivities. A bit 'tired,' I'm told. A bit blotto is more like it. Martin, you shall take the reverend's seat, alright?"

"Can I say no?" asked Martin.

"No!" responded the adults in unison.

"Bernard, please show Martin to his table," said the woman.

"Certainly, Miss Sample," replied Bernard. "Right this way, Master Van Buren!"

Martin glowered at Bernard as they walked away and said, "This is going to be a *very* expensive night for you, Bernard."

* * *

Martin had been seated at the head table on a number of occasions in the past, but always as his grandmother's escort. His participation at the benefit of the Hammertoe Foundation was his first without a companion, and he was unsure how to interact with his tablemates. His neighbor, a well-dressed middle-aged man who also appeared to be alone, seemed to sense his unease and initiated a conversation with him.

"So, what brings you out in your monkey suit tonight, son?" said the man.

Martin decided that the best course would be to stick with Bernard's bogus story. "I was going to come to dinner with my grandmother, but her dog was eaten by a lizard."

"Her dog was eaten by a lizard? That must've been some lizard. Or not much of a dog. So you're here on your own? Why didn't you cancel too? There's no way you would have caught me going to one of these things when I was your age."

"I didn't have a choice," replied Martin with a frown. "But if you don't like these parties, then why are you here?"

"Not for the food or entertainment, that's for sure. I mean, Barry Boca? He might have been big for a few weeks in the seventies, but now he's usually drunk before he even hits the stage. By the way, my name is Mount. Nick Mount."

"I'm Martin. Are you here because you have hammertoes?"

The man laughed. "No, I don't have hammertoes. Listen, can you keep a secret? I'm here because I sell real estate, and everyone who attends events like this is a prospective client. Only the richest of the rich will pay for tickets to things like this. Most of them also give money for hammertoe research, God help us. There is no more lucrative business in Palm Beach than real estate, so attending these events is a professional obligation as far as I'm concerned."

"Do you go to a lot of these things?" asked Martin.

"Usually three nights a week during the season. Tomorrow night I'll be attending the 30th annual Goiter Gala at the Breakers. Now *that* should be fun," said the man as he displayed a crooked smile.

"Do you know these other people at our table?" asked Martin.

"I don't know them, but I met them a little while ago." Nick Mount lowered his voice. "The couple to your right, the guy sold his company for $115 million. He invented the remote-control toilet seat."

"A remote-control toilet seat? Why would anybody want that?"

"A lot of people do, apparently, if somebody bought his company for $115 million. In fact, most of the people who buy his toilet seats live in Palm Beach or Tokyo. Sticklers for comfort and hygiene, I guess. A bit much if you ask me, but to each his own. The woman he's with is his wife. He married her just after he sold his company. Pretty hot little number. He lives in a seven-bedroom house on El Vedado and he's not looking to move, so I'm not going to bother with him."

"Who is the man next to her?" asked Martin.

"Oh, that guy's a jeweler on Worth Avenue. He's just trying to make some sales tonight too. The girl with him is a model. All of her jewelry is for sale. Forget about them."

"So he isn't rich?"

"Not Palm Beach rich, if you know what I mean, although he does own a Lamborghini."

"Why would somebody own a Lamborghini in Palm Beach? Isn't the speed limit 30 miles an hour?"

"There's really no reason to own a Lamborghini in Palm Beach, or a Ferrari, a Bentley, or a Hummer for that matter. It's all about image and status and trying too hard to impress people who have so much money that they really can't be impressed."

Nick Mount stopped to take a sip of white wine. "Now, the couple to my left is interesting. She's the one who made the fortune, not him. Get this; she designs clothing for dogs! Seasonal things, like Santa Claus outfits for Christmas, Easter bunny outfits for Easter. Also dog collars with semiprecious stones. The women in Palm Beach can't get enough of this stuff, and she's selling these things for thousands of dollars! Maybe that's the business I should be in. She lives in an eight-bedroom Mizner house on South Ocean Boulevard and she's not looking to move either. I guess I just didn't have any luck with my table assignment tonight. Although it's nice to have someone normal to talk to, even if he is a kid."

The man paused as he inspected Martin and then asked, "How old are you, 12?"

"Ten," said Martin with pride.

"Wow, you're only ten years old? You're pretty mature for your age."

"And what about that couple?" asked Martin, pointing across the table to a very tall, very skinny woman and a very short, very stout man.

"Didn't your mother ever teach you not to point?" Mount asked Martin.

"No. And besides, she's in London."

"Oh, so that's why your grandmother is looking after you. Your grandmother who is missing in action."

Martin was startled by Mount's comment, but he quickly realized that he had simply used a figure of speech.

"So, that couple across from us. She is Her Royal and Serene Highness Princess Megan of Norway and he is her husband, Prince Olaf."

The princess looked up when she heard her name. Having given up her lifelong battle to incorporate polysyllabic words into her conversations, she simply smiled and said, "Hi."

"Hi," said Martin. Emboldened by the supportive presence of his neighbor, he decided to try to initiate a conversation with Her Royal and Serene Highness. "I was in Norway once when I was five. The food was gross. How do you eat it?"

The princess was put off by the content of his remark and the need to respond intelligibly. "I'm not from there. I'm from here."

"But he said your name is . . . what was it? The Royal Latrine Highness something something of Norway."

"I'm not from there. I'm from here," she repeated.

"Is he from Norway?" asked Martin, pointing at her rotund husband.

"Yes, he was born there."

"Well, does he go to Norway all the time?"

"No, he has not been there since he was born."

Martin was confused. "So how come if you're from here and he hasn't been to Norway since he was born . . ."

Mount decided to intervene in the interests of international diplomacy. "Martin, you're too young to be able to read adult publications—"

"I can read fine."

"—but Their Royal and Serene Highnesses have been profiled in many popular magazines. In fact, they were on the cover of last week's *Hello* magazine." The princess beamed with pride. "Everybody knows that Prince Olaf was exiled from Norway as a newborn baby due to certain indiscretions committed by his father King Haakon the Hopeless—"

"Never proven!" squealed the prince despite his mouthful of food.

"Never proven, you're absolutely right, Your Highness," Mount continued, while simultaneously winking his right eye at Martin, "and we all support them in their ongoing struggle to reclaim the throne of their beloved homeland."

"I will not live there," said the princess. "It's too cold. And the boy is right. The food is gross. It's all fish. Cream and fish."

"See?" said Martin, who received an elbow to his ribs from Nick Mount.

"But darling," said the prince to his wife, "wouldn't you want to be by my side when I return to rule over my homeland? My Norwegian lessons are coming along so well. I'll let you redecorate the palace."

"No."

The prince looked over at Mount and Martin and said with embarrassment, "Oh, the struggles we royals face! You commoners have no idea!"

Nick Mount allowed that last statement to pass and seized on a business opportunity. "Hey, speaking of royals," he said to the prince, "there's a gorgeous estate a few blocks north of Royal Palm Way that just came on the market. They're asking $20 million, but I'm sure that price is negotiable." He paused and glanced to his left and right and then whispered, "The husband is under indictment." In a louder voice, he continued, "Why don't you let me show it to you tomorrow?"

Chapter Twelve

The telephone woke Bernard at 8:20 the following morning, long before his alarm clock had been scheduled to sound. He had arrived home at his small but tidy apartment in West Palm Beach only six hours previously because the Hammertoe Foundation fund-raiser had ended late. He had hoped to have a chance to recover from his jet lag, but it was not to be.

Bernard reached out to pick up the phone and rolled off the couch onto the floor, forgetting that he had given Martin his bed for the night. He was certainly looking forward to the return of the boy's grandmother, assuming that she was actually going to return, that is. He had decided that he was a little too young for parenthood.

Bernard crawled over to the table and picked up the phone after the fifth ring.

"Hello?" he answered groggily.

"Is this a Mr. Bernard Dauphin?"

"Yes, who is calling?"

"This is Rex Randolph. I am the lead architect on Margaret Van Buren's guesthouse renovation. She asked me to call
you to invite you to join me at the ACES meeting this morning, where I'll be presenting her plans for town approval."

"Excuse me? ACES? I'm sorry, I'm a little sleepy and I
don't understand."

"ACES. The Aesthetics of Construction Engineering
Subcommittee. Mrs. Van Buren requested that you join me at
the ACES meeting. She said that you were young and just
starting out and she felt that the experience would be good
for you. Personally, these meetings are difficult enough without some novice hanging around, but it was important to her,
so that's why I'm calling you."

"When did Mrs. Van Buren ask you to call me? I've been
looking for her, but no one seems to know where she is."

"She called me last week. I haven't needed to speak with
her since then, so I couldn't tell you where she might be right
now."

Bernard struggled to focus on the conversation, his eye-
lids drooping with fatigue. "What is this ACES? You say
there's a meeting that I should attend?"

"Wow, you really are inexperienced. ACES is *everything*,
young man. When you're planning to build, you can't even
blow your nose without ACES approval. I'm scheduled to
present at 10:40 this morning and I'm calling to see if you'll
be there."

"This morning? That's not a lot of notice. She told you
about this last week but you waited until this morning to call
me?"

"You weren't exactly my highest priority, son."

"Have you called Oliver Booth yet?"

"Who's Oliver Booth?"

"He owns an antiques store on . . . just off Worth Avenue. We've been working together on the furniture plan for Mrs. Van Buren's guesthouse. Although I've been doing most of the work."

"I don't know anything about any Oliver Booth. In fact, now that you mention it, Mrs. Van Buren told me to invite you and only you. So there's your answer."

Bernard stretched. "So you present at 10:40 this morning?" he asked.

"Yes, but be there at ten o'clock, please. That's when the meeting starts. You never know if they're going to move items around on the agenda. And you don't want to miss the beginning. I think you'll find it pretty entertaining. I'll see you at 10:00 at Town Hall. 360 South County Road."

Bernard hung up the phone and glanced over at the sleeping boy. "Martin, it's time to wake up," he said. "We have a meeting to attend."

* * *

The Aesthetics of Construction Engineering Subcommittee of the town of Palm Beach, or ACES, consists of seven duly elected members, typically men, who themselves are known informally as the Aces. In fact, the members tend to call each other Ace when they meet on social occasions, both during their tenure on the subcommittee and even long after their typically forced retirement from public service.

ACES meets once every month and serves as the arbiter of aesthetics with regard to property development in Palm Beach. While the Town Council concerns itself with more concrete matters related to zoning and building codes, ACES is responsible for decisions regarding building style and landscaping, ranging from the overall look of a project to the smallest detail of bathroom design. The members of ACES have varying credentials as arbiters of taste, ranging from degrees in dentistry to expertise in the art and science of dry cleaning. A lack of any specific training in architecture and design in no way dissuades the members of this august body from rendering swift and frequently harsh verdicts on the matters brought before them.

Although there is no specific age requirement for membership on ACES, a casual glance at the members would suggest that a minimum of 65 years of life experience would be essential before one would be considered suitably wizened for service. ACES members do not wear the austere black robes of judges, although that would not be inappropriate given the severity of their decisions. Instead, they tend toward a uniform of sport jackets and slacks in a rainbow of pastels. For instance, lime green slacks could be matched with a pink sport coat, or a yellow sport coat might be matched with tartan pants. All of these outfits are topped off with neckties that depict the accoutrements of many of the leisure activities that are so popular on the island, such as golf balls, tennis racquets, and—although few town members have ever actually sat upon a horse—polo mallets.

Rex Randolph, Bernard, and Martin were sitting together toward the back of the spectator section of the Town Council chambers when the session began. Horatio Flagg, the chairman of ACES, opened the meeting by leading the members in the Pledge of Allegiance and then a prayer.

Bernard looked on, confused. "Isn't there some rule about separating church and state in this country?" he asked Randolph in a low voice. "Are they really supposed to be saying a prayer to open a government meeting?"

"They can do anything they want. They're ACES. Besides, they call it an invocation, not a prayer, so they would probably get by on a technicality."

Chairman Flagg called for the first item on the agenda.

"Item number one, new construction at 264 El Brillo," announced the clerk. "The property is owned by Mr. and Mrs. Johnson Sinclair, and the presentation will be made by Filbert Boone, of Boone Architectural Group. Mr. Boone?"

Filbert Boone stepped up to the lectern and said, "Thank you, it is my pleasure to be here."

"And it's always our pleasure to review your projects, Mr. Boone," Flagg responded. "Your reputation precedes you. Not to mention the fact that you recently finished a design for my new house. By the way, my check's in the mail, Filbert."

"That's what they all say, Horatio, that's what they all say! No, no, I know you're good for it!" Boone paused to allow himself to recover from his fit of laughter. "I am here today to present a preliminary plan for an estate to be located at 264 El Brillo. You have all had my drawings for a few weeks, and I believe it's fair to say that I have met with each of you ex parte, am I correct?"

Grouped mumblings of assent were heard.

"Good, so none of this should be unfamiliar to you." Boone turned toward a large watercolor painting supported by an easel. "Now, as you can see in this rendering, my firm has designed a beautiful Mediterranean-style home. On the exterior, we will have a traditional Spanish barrel tile roof and a stucco facade that will be painted a warm pinkish hue. To enhance the splendor of the view for the homeowners when they are inside their home, we are proposing a succession of picture windows that will be 6 feet in height and 12 feet in width. Moving to the interior of the house—"

"Mr. Boone, excuse me, but I have a question," interjected Chip "Skip" Dickinson, who at 62 was one of the younger members of ACES. "Those windows are certainly beautiful, but aren't they a bit large? I mean, how will they stand up to hurricane-force winds?"

Boone offered a forced smile. "Mr. Dickinson, although my initial inclination is to respectfully suggest that the strength of the windows is an issue outside the purview of ACES because it is a matter of building code, I anticipate that you will be reassured to know that we will be fabricating steel plates that will be bolted to the window frames to protect against any damage in the event that a storm approaches."

"Wouldn't those be a bit heavy?" continued Dickinson, oblivious to Boone's growing irritation. "I calculate that each of the steel plates would be 72 square feet in surface area. I hope the homeowners attend the gym regularly!"

Boone's patience was wearing thin with the persistent inquiries of this young upstart. "Mr. Dickinson, the homeowners already have in place a large staff who would be responsible for securing those steel plates. And let me specifically inform you that their senior houseboy was the welterweight boxing champion of Ecuador in 1999. He could install those panels with his bandana tied over his eyes."

"Thank you for your satisfactory response, Mr. Boone. Please continue," said Chairman Flagg while frowning at Dickinson.

"As I was saying," Boone continued with a brief scowl, "the interior of this house is dedicated to one simple notion: luxury. Luxury in the most expensive . . . er, I mean expansive sense of the word. Marble floors, Venetian plaster walls, pecky cypress beams supporting the second floor. In terms of function, there will be seven bedrooms, eight bathrooms, and a four-car garage. There will also be separate servants' quarters situated close to the rear property line. I would suggest that the drawings otherwise speak for themselves. Any questions?" Boone glanced at his watch to remind the members of ACES of the value of his time and the need for a hasty resolution of this matter.

The chairman looked up and said, "Yes, Mr. Boone, I have a question. Why don't we have another ex parte communication at the bar at Ta-boó after ACES concludes its work today?" The entire room broke into laughter, including Filbert Boone.

"That would be aces, Ace!" replied Boone.

"Well, I would suggest that this project is straightforward," continued Flagg, "and in my opinion, it would be a lovely addition to Palm Beach. Do I hear a motion to approve the plans as submitted?"

"So moved!" shouted a member.

"Would someone like to second the motion?" asked Flagg.

"Second!"

"All in favor say aye."

Many voices were raised in assent.

"Any misguided nays?"

Silence.

"The plans are approved. Congratulations on another beautiful presentation, Mr. Boone," concluded Flagg. "See you at Ta-boó at noon!" he added in a stage whisper.

Bernard leaned over to Rex Randolph and said, "That wasn't so bad. Everyone seems to be really respectful of each other."

"Just wait," Randolph replied.

Martin jabbed Bernard in the side with his elbow. "Hey, this is really boring."

Bernard rubbed his side where he had been poked. "Yes, I know, Martin, it's boring for me too, but your grandmother wanted me to be here to listen to the presentation of her plans, and if I'm here, you have to be here."

"I was making money wasting my time yesterday. Today I'm wasting my time for nothing."

"Well, just keep listening, maybe you'll learn something."

"I want $20."

"I don't have $20."

"I take Euros too."

"Shush."

"Let's move to the next item on the agenda," said Chairman Flagg.

"Item number two, new construction at 237 Via del Lago," said the clerk. "The property is owned by a Mr. Sonny Skatapolis, and the presentation will be made by Julio Condenado, of Condenado Construction of Boca Raton."

Julio Condenado took his place at the lectern and said, "Gentlemen, I am pleased and honored to be making my first presentation before the Aesthetics of Construction Engineering Subcommittee today. I will be describing our plans for the development of 237 Via del Lago."

"Have there been any ex parte communications?" interrupted Flagg.

Mumbled grunts in the negative were heard.

"The stenographer will note that there have been no ex parte communications."

"Mr. Flagg, I had actually hoped to meet with the ACES members prior to today's session," interjected Condenado, "but despite the repeated messages that I left, none of my telephone calls were returned."

"Señor Con ... den ... an ... do," replied Flagg, phonetically but incorrectly, "I'm sure you must realize that we are all very busy men. Please begin your presentation. We have a very full agenda today."

"Absolutely, sir. As reflected in the plans that I sent each of you a few weeks ago, the owner's intention is to build a Mediterranean-style home—"

"Excuse me, sir," interrupted Flagg in horror, "did you say Mediterranean style?"

"Yes, Mediterranean style. I was going to say that—"

"Don't you think there's enough Mediterranean-style construction going on in Palm Beach already, sir?"

"Well, actually, no. In fact, all of the remaining houses on Via del Lago are Mediterranean in style, and I'm sure you must remember that you approved Mr. Filbert Boone's plans for a Mediterranean-style house just a few minutes ago."

Chairman Flagg was outraged. "Sir, we do not need to be reminded of our actions. With all due respect, you are no Filbert Boone, and it is our charge to guide the development and redevelopment of Palm Beach as we see fit. I don't know how they do things in your country—"

"I'm from Jacksonville, sir," replied Condenado with growing anxiety.

"—and frankly, I don't care. Now, let me ask my fellow ACES members, am I incorrect in stating that new projects need to move away from the Mediterranean—"

"But Addison Mizner—"

"And you are also no Addison Mizner, sir!" responded Flagg in a loud voice. "Now, I move that the members of ACES reject the plans as drawn and suggest that Señor

Condenado consult with his team in Boca Raton . . ." Flagg paused and threw a knowing glance at each of the members of ACES, "and return with an alternative concept. Personally, I have always loved Tudor homes. They're very cozy and they make me think of Shakespeare. Perhaps a thatched roof would be an interesting visual feature. All in favor?"

A loud chorus of ayes was heard.

"Opposed?"

Silence.

"So moved. Return with plans for a Tudor-style house. Good day, sir."

"But a thatched roof would not hold up during hurricane season!" pleaded Condenado.

"A matter for the Town Council, not ACES, sir. Perhaps you should review that issue with them before we see you again in our chamber. Again, good day to you, sir."

Julio Condenado left the room in tears.

Rex Randolph smiled and turned to Bernard, who looked shocked. "See what I mean?" he said.

"You're not from Boca Raton, are you?" asked Bernard.

"No," laughed Rex Randolph, "and I think we'll be fine. But you never know."

"What is the next matter on the agenda?" asked the chairman.

"Item number three, a renovation at 276 Via Bellaria," announced the clerk. "The property is owned by Mrs. Margaret Van Buren, and the presentation will be made by Rex Randolph, of Randolph Associates."

"That's me," said Randolph as he stood up and walked to the lectern. "Gentlemen," he began, nodding to the members of ACES, "and ma'am," he added, acknowledging the stenographer, who smiled, "I am Rex Randolph, and I am pleased to be back before you to present our plans for a renovation of the guesthouse at 276 Via Bellaria. Now, I did not meet with any of you ex parte, but I hope you found the plans and renderings that I had delivered to you informative."

"Yes, Mr. Randolph, they were clear and complete as always," responded Flagg. "Please proceed."

"Well, this is a relatively straightforward project. It is primarily an interior renovation, with certain non-load-bearing walls being removed to create larger rooms that will permit Mrs. Van Buren's adult children and their offspring to use the space more effectively. Regarding exterior changes, we will be adding an open loggia to the lower floor to provide more outdoor play space. The loggia will not encroach on the required setbacks, and its design will be in a style compatible with that of the remainder of the guesthouse as well as the main house. As you can see in the renderings, it, too, will be typically Mediterranean."

Startled, Bernard looked up, concerned that Randolph's use of that forbidden word would be his downfall. He was surprised when Flagg said, "Very nice, Mr. Randolph, very simple and clean and appropriate."

Dickinson raised his hand and said, "Excuse me, Mr. Randolph, but I was wondering how the interior design of the house would marry the proposed classically Mediterranean sensibility with the demands of family life. I mean, my own grandchildren really shouldn't even be allowed into civilized company."

Bernard glanced at Martin and smirked.

Randolph hesitated. "Well, that's a reasonable question, I suppose, but I'm not sure I can be helpful because I haven't been involved in the interior design meetings." He reflected and then brightened. "Actually, there is someone here today who might be able to answer your question. Bernard, would you step forward, please?"

Bernard pointed toward himself and mouthed the word, "Me?" Randolph nodded. Bernard stepped up to the lectern and waited expectantly.

"Well?" said Chairman Flagg.

"Well what, sir?" responded Bernard.

"Well, what are you going to tell the members about the interior design of Mrs. Van Buren's guesthouse? Speak up, boy!"

"I'm not really a professional decorator. I wouldn't know where to—"

"I'll make it simple for you, son," said Flagg. "Have you purchased any furniture yet?"

"Well, yes, but—"

"Then tell us about it, boy! It's a simple question!"

Rex Randolph leaned forward and whispered to Bernard, "You'd better start talking or we're going to be in big trouble. And when I say we, I mean you."

Bernard took a deep breath and said, "Alright, well, we just returned from Paris where we were shopping at the Marché aux Puces, the flea market . . ."

Flagg smiled and said, "I'm sure you weren't shopping in some flea market, son, not for a person like Margaret Van Buren. Now please describe some of your purchases to give us . . ."

The chairman was interrupted by the sound of a disturbance at the back of the room. Bernard turned to see a police officer running up the aisle. "Excuse me, please, I must get through. Mr. Flagg, sir, I apologize for the interruption, but there's an emergency. There's a riot on Worth Avenue. Well, not ON Worth Avenue, just around the corner at the end of

Worth Avenue. All official town business has been ordered to cease in the interests of ensuring public safety."

"A riot, you say? In Palm Beach? On Worth Avenue?"

"Just around the corner at the end of Worth Avenue, sir," responded the officer.

"What is this world coming to?" muttered Horatio Flagg. "Alright, let's just tie up this one loose end and then we'll adjourn. I move, and second the motion, that we approve Mrs. Van Buren's plans as presented and thus end this session. All in favor?"

The members shouted their assent.

"Alright, I would like to invite everybody to join me in my office. Let's turn on the television and find out what's going on."

The members scurried off the dais, leaving Bernard and Rex Randolph at the lectern looking confused. Bernard turned and said, "I guess that was a lucky break, wasn't it?"

"You aren't much of a public speaker, are you, Bernard?"

"Well, no, I suppose I'm not, but I wasn't prepared to be called up in front of the committee."

Randolph smiled. "Don't worry, I have a feeling you'll have other chances in the future. Come on. Let's go find out who is rioting on Worth Avenue. Maybe there's a sample sale in one of the shops."

Bernard laughed and then reflected on the clerk's announcement. The riot was not *on* Worth Avenue; it was just around the corner *at the end of* Worth Avenue. Since it was unlikely that a riot would ever begin in a barbershop, that left only Oliver Booth's establishment. And, as Bernard well knew, it was exceedingly likely that Oliver would be the cause of a riot.

CHAPTER THIRTEEN

Bernard, Martin, and Rex Randolph left Town Hall, walked down South County Road, and turned right onto Worth Avenue. They increased their pace as they began to hear a commotion in the distance. Passing store after store, they saw shoppers' faces pressed against the glass, their expressions quizzical, suggesting a desire for someone, anyone, other than themselves to handle whatever situation had arisen, particularly if it otherwise meant an interruption of their purchases and an unwelcome venture out into the intense noontime sun.

As it became clear that the commotion was centered on Oliver's shop, Bernard began to expect both the worst and an entertaining spectacle. At the end of Worth Avenue, they turned the corner and immediately found themselves at the edge of a mob of at least a hundred people who seemed to be straining to move forward to enter the store. Bernard wondered what Oliver had said on this occasion to offend so many people at one time. He asked Rex Randolph to look after Martin while he attempted to negotiate his way through the crowd.

"Excuse me, pardon me, excuse me—"

"Hey, don't shove!" yelled a woman as Bernard inched his way forward. "Wait your turn!"

"My turn?" asked Bernard. "Is this a line?"

"Sort of. I think it becomes a line toward the front. But it will only become a line if people like you wait their turn. Now step back!" She jabbed Bernard in the ribs with her very pointy elbow.

"Hey!" yelled Bernard, rubbing his side. He retreated to the outside of the mob and looked for an opening. Noticing that the crowd was composed almost entirely of women, and quite well-dressed women at that, he stepped toward an older man who was standing nearby and watching with a bemused expression. Bernard asked him what was happening.

The man laughed. "I can't quite put it into words. You have to see for yourself." He pointed to the edge of the crowd and said, "Go around there to the left side of the front door. It looks like you can kind of wedge yourself in and get a good look. But be careful. These women are dangerous."

Bernard walked in the direction the man had pointed and found a narrow opening between the women and the facade of the building. Approaching the shop's window, he noticed that the women who had successfully navigated their way to the front of the crowd were on their knees, weeping.

"What in God's name is going on here?" he whispered to himself as he looked up to see Oliver's sweaty, blotchy face and leering grin next to the painting of Saint Gisella in the front window of the store. Bernard realized that somehow these women had discovered, or had been told, that the painting of Saint Gisella weeps and that it might somehow work miracles for them. Thinking quickly, he pushed his way toward the front door, shouting, "Coming through, clerk of the shop, collector of Saint Gisella's tears."

Hearing this, the crowd parted. Bernard quickly made his way inside to speak with Oliver, who was standing next to a large, elaborately carved wooden bucket filled with $100 bills.

"Oliver, what is going on here?" he asked. "This is out of control. There are even television crews outside." Bernard walked over to Oliver's desk and turned on his television set. He flipped to a local station and a view from outside the shop came on the screen. "Don't you understand? You must stop this."

"Come to rain on my little parade, eh, boy? Well, it's not going to happen," said Oliver. "A little publicity will just make my venture even more successful. My prediction came true. This painting is going to provide me with my oh-so-well-deserved nest egg."

"Where did all of this money come from, Oliver?"

"From these unfortunate women, Bernard. Oh, I do so feel their pain!" he cried melodramatically. "They understand, oh they understand so well, what Saint Gisella can do for them! These poor women, troubled by disorders of the skin, seeking relief from their blessed saint!"

Bernard looked through the window at the faces of the kneeling women. "Disorders of the skin? What disorders of the skin? They look fine to me. I mean, their faces seem a little tight, but—"

"Exactly, my neophytic little friend, exactly!" said Oliver. "For so many years, women have sought consolation through scalpels and syringes, but no more! Now they need simply come to my retreat—"

"Retreat?"

"Yes. My shop has been transformed into a bit of a spa. I have renamed it the Retreat of Saint Gisella. As I was saying, these women need only come to my retreat, demonstrate the seriousness of their commitment by making a small contribution of at least $100 for the upkeep of the painting—"

"What upkeep is there on a painting?"

"Well, not on the painting itself, but perhaps toward my own upkeep as protector of the painting," replied Oliver. "They will then be able to rest assured that their conditions will remit. Just think, Bernard, no more surgery, no more Botox parties! Oh, the blessed relief for these poor unfortunates!"

"Oliver," Bernard whispered, "you must realize that this is fraud. Paintings do not weep, and I doubt that there is even a Saint Gisella."

Oliver looked at him, horrified. "Heretic!" he yelled. "Unbeliever!" He turned to the assembled women. "Friends, demonstrate your respect for Saint Gisella and expel this infidel from our midst!"

The women rose as one, and those who had successfully navigated their way into the shop gladly gave up their prime positions near the painting to dig their well-manicured nails into Bernard's arms and pull him outside, believing that this show of devotion would bring them greater rewards than simple prayer. In just a few seconds, Bernard found himself back on the edge of the crowd near Martin and Rex Randolph, the recipient of a hundred menacing stares.

"Um, Bernard?" said Martin. "I think you're bleeding."

"Yes, I know," said Bernard, looking at the many tiny cuts that marked both of his arms. "And my ribs hurt too."

"You couldn't have paid me to go in there, son," said Randolph. "Was I right? Was it a sample sale?"

"Not exactly."

In the distance, they heard the sound of sirens.

"This should be interesting," said Bernard.

The crowd stepped back grudgingly as a police car pulled up to the curb. Two officers from the Palm Beach Police Department stepped out of the car and walked toward the shop, the crowd eyeing them suspiciously.

The officers entered the shop and found Oliver, who quickly displayed his most ingratiating smile. "Yes, officers, what can I do for you? Are you in the market for antiques? Can I bring you a glass of water or a snack?"

The officers ignored Oliver's offers. "What is your name, sir?" one asked.

"Oliver Booth, officer."

"And you are the owner of this shop?"

"Yes, well, I lease the space, but I am the man in charge."

"Can you explain what is going on here?"

Oliver thought carefully about how best to respond. "Certainly. You see, I recently returned from a trip to Paris, France, where I purchased many wonderful antiques. Among them is the beautiful painting that you see in the window, a painting of a saint. Apparently, and much to my surprise, this saint has many followers in our community. In the spirit of religious tolerance, I thought it would be proper to display this sacred relic to permit them to honor their beloved martyr. I have certainly done my best to keep the sidewalk and road clear."

"It sure doesn't look like it," said the second officer.

"Mr. Booth, what is this bucket of cash doing here?" asked the first officer. "Do you understand that you would be a sitting duck for a burglar? It would really be in your best interest to invest in a more modern bookkeeping system."

"Oh yes, officer, you're absolutely right. I absolutely must purchase a strongbox. Now, if you'll excuse me—"

"Not just yet, Mr. Booth. Tell me, do you have a permit to hold a religious service on your property?"

"A religious service? What religious service?"

"How else would you describe the activity around your shop, sir?"

"Oh, no, it's certainly not a religious service. It's just a group of women who have come together—"

"Exactly, sir. Town ordinances state that you must have a permit to hold a religious service, which is defined as an organized meeting of two or more people for the purpose of worship. From the look of it, this crowd is more disorganized than organized, but I'll need to write you a ticket and then disperse the crowd."

"Disperse the crowd, oh no!" cried Oliver. "But I was just beginning to make some . . . how much will the ticket cost?"

"A first violation will be $50, sir."

"Oh, well, only $50! Officers, I do apologize for my unintentional misdeed and for taking you away from your more important duties to protect the good people of Palm Beach."

The officer finished writing the ticket. "Sir, all of our duties are equally important. Now please see that this does not happen again. The fine for a second violation increases to $100."

Oliver was relieved. "Yes, officer, of course, I'll be more careful."

As the policemen walked out of the shop, they attempted to herd the women into a manageable group that could be led away, but it was an arduous process as the women continued to weep and reach out toward the painting of Saint Gisella. Ten minutes later, only Bernard, Martin, and Rex Randolph remained outside the shop, while Oliver stood in the doorway beaming at them.

"Well, Bernard, are you finally impressed with me?" asked Oliver. "The ticket will cost me $50, but I made thousands today. Thousands! And all thanks to Mrs. Van Buren, who subsidized my purchase of the painting of the benevolent and beloved Saint Gisella."

Rex Randolph raised an eyebrow at Oliver's comment.

"If you'll excuse me, I shall now bathe," continued Oliver. "Although I am inclined to wash off the tears of those unfortunate women with my own tears of joy, I tend to think that soap will be more effective. I shall also be enjoying a glass of champagne and closing for the day. Or perhaps for the week! Good-bye."

Oliver turned to walk into the shop, failing to realize that the marble floor had become treacherously slick with the tears of Saint Gisella's acolytes. His feet flew out from under him and he landed on Napoleon, who had been sleeping soundly following the many hours that he had spent cowering in a corner of the shop to avoid the heaving mob of women. Awakened with a start, Napoleon did what any dog would instinctively do. He clamped his powerful jaws down on the hindquarters of the beast that had threatened him. Regrettably, that beast turned out to be Oliver and the hindquarters were his. In the few seconds that it took Napoleon to realize what he had done and release his prey, Oliver had lost a small chunk of flabby flesh and, as he looked up to see Bernard, Martin, and Rex Randolph looking down on him, a large measure of his pride.

* * *

The paramedics arrived just moments after Bernard's 9-1-1 call to find Oliver lying on the ground and bleeding from the large hole Napoleon had torn in the seat of his pants. Bernard's efforts to provide them with a detailed description of the incident were punctuated by Oliver's moans, pleas for painkillers, and demands that Napoleon be put to sleep. Instead, the paramedics hesitantly assessed Oliver's posterior, loaded him onto a stretcher and into the ambulance, patted Napoleon, and then drove off, laughing.

There is no hospital in Palm Beach, so Oliver was taken over the North Bridge to Our Most Vengeful Savior Medical Center. Vengeful Savior is a 500-bed public hospital located in the heart of West Palm Beach, and for that reason it tends to cater to drifters and the indigent rather than the moneyed class from the island. The exotic clientele of Vengeful Savior draws many skilled clinicians, however, who see it as a fruitful opportunity to conduct research into rare diseases. Those same clinicians also find that it is quite lucrative to restrict their private practices to the residents of Palm Beach, who prefer to be treated for their minor ailments in a more discreet setting and then transported once a year to the Mayo Clinic for comprehensive examinations.

The atmosphere in the emergency room of Vengeful Savior, like emergency rooms everywhere, tends to range from a state of mild disorganization to utter chaos. On the day of Oliver's admission, it fell somewhere in between, the staff having just begun to regain some semblance of control after caring for a man who had walked in the front door an hour earlier with an axe lodged in his skull. That unfortunate fellow, who had been attacked following a less-than-legitimate victory in a game of dominoes outside a nearby Publix grocery store, had required the services of most of the emergency room team, particularly housekeeping, which had made the arrival of Oliver with his bitten bottom that much more unwelcome.

Rex Randolph pulled up at the entrance to Vengeful Savior's emergency room, and Bernard and Martin climbed out of his sports car. As Randolph drove off, they entered and inquired about Oliver at the registration desk.

"You're here for Booth? What a baby," said the clerk. "I haven't seen anybody cry like that since I worked with preterm infants." She looked at her logbook. "You'll find him in bed 8; just go through the swinging doors." She handed Bernard a box of tissues and added, chuckling, "Here, take these. He'll probably need them!"

Bernard and Martin turned to walk into the patient treatment area.

"Hold it!" shouted the clerk. "That child can't go in with you. You have to be 16 or older to visit with patients. There are some gross things back there."

Realizing that he couldn't leave Martin alone in the waiting room, Bernard thought quickly and said, "Um, Mr. Booth is my employer and this is his son. Martin is very upset about his father's injuries, aren't you, Martin?"

"Yes, I'm very upset," replied Martin in a bored monotone.

"You say this child is Oliver Booth's son?" asked the clerk. "Doubtful. Very doubtful. There's not even a resemblance, you know."

"Um, Martin's adopted," said Bernard.

Seizing on an opportunity for mischief, Martin cried out, "I'm adopted? Nobody ever told me I was adopted! Who are my real parents? I want my real mommy and daddy!" Martin could barely hide his glee at having been given such a wonderful chance to torture Bernard.

Aghast, Bernard quickly responded, "Now, Martin, being adopted can be a wonderful thing." He reached into his pocket for his wallet. "You wouldn't have wanted to stay in Iceland, now, would you? Since you asked, I believe I have a photograph of your biological father, if I can just find it. Ah, yes, here it is."

Bernard pretended to show Martin a photograph in the palm of his hand, which actually concealed yet another in a continuing series of $20 bills. "See, Martin, isn't he handsome? You'll probably be quite handsome too when you're a grown-up."

Pleased to have been shown the engraving of Andrew Jackson on the banknote, which he quickly snatched, Martin said, "I'm starting to feel better, but I want to see another picture of my daddy."

The clerk watched the spectacle unfolding in front of her, expressionless. Scenes like this were the rule rather than the exception in the emergency room.

"I believe I have another picture of your father in my wallet," said Bernard, as he pulled out a second $20 bill, "and I promise that I'll find you another one when we get home if you're a good boy. Alright?"

"You promise?" asked Martin. "I love my real daddy. He's so handsome. Was he the president of the United States?"

Bernard rolled his eyes at the clerk and said, "These kids and their imaginations! Alright, Martin, let's go!"

Bernard and Martin began walking toward the curtain again as Martin pocketed his money.

"Excuse me, where do you think you're going?" asked the clerk.

Surprised, Bernard said, "Well, to see Mr. Booth, of course. What do you think we—"

"I told you, the child can't visit unless he's 16 or older."

"But I told you, he's Mr. Booth's son—"

"Listen, I don't care if his father is the pope, he's not getting past me until he's 16 or older. Why don't you just have him sit down in one of those empty seats over there by the restrooms? I'll keep my eye on him while you're visiting. Just don't be long."

Realizing that he didn't have any alternative, Bernard agreed and told Martin that he would be back in five minutes. He went through the swinging doors and began to look for bed 8.

* * *

Oliver had been assigned to a first-year medical student, who had asked him to disrobe, don a strikingly undersized hospital gown, and then attach a leather harness around his waist. With Herculean effort, the medical student, unaided, had successfully managed to attach Oliver, bottom end up, to a traction assembly that was mounted over his bed and hoist him into the air. And so, having found bed 8 and passed through the privacy curtain, Bernard was shocked to be greeted by an eye-level view of Oliver's plump and painful posterior that the hospital gown was insufficient to hide.

"Oliver?"

"Who's there? Come around here so I can see you."

One unfortunate consequence of Oliver's positioning was that, while others could see more of him than he would have liked, he was able to see only a chart positioned on the wall directly in front of him that outlined—in Spanish, with cartoons—the primary symptoms of a variety of sexually transmitted diseases. After only a few minutes of staring at that chart, he had grown tired of Luis and Carlotta and their *enfermedades*.

"Oliver, it's me, Bernard."

"Oh, it's you. Well, I have nothing to say to you."

"How are you feeling?"

"La-di-da, there's no one there, I'm all alone."

"Oliver, that's not very mature."

"Oh, what's that noise? Is it somebody speaking? No, I think the fellow in the next bed just farted."

"Oliver, why are you being so difficult? What did I do?"

"What did you do? What did *you* do?" Oliver struggled to turn his body so he could face Bernard, but the traction device would not permit it. As he wiggled his exposed buttocks in the air unpleasantly, he vented at Luis and Carlotta. "I don't know how you did it, but you're responsible for me being here in this mortifying position. How did you get Napoleon to bite me? Did you step on his foot?"

"I had nothing to do with this, Oliver. You slipped on a wet floor and you fell on your dog. What did you expect him to do, lick your face? You're not exactly slim, you know."

"I don't need any sarcastic comments about my weight, Bernard, especially right now. I'm feeling rather exposed, and there doesn't seem to be any real hope of my receiving actual medical care. That medical student hung me up here like a side of beef at least an hour ago and nobody has been by since. Except for you, of course, but you're useless."

"Would you like me to see if I can find a doctor for you, Oliver?"

"That would be quite civil of you. And it's the least you could do. But before you go, could you find a sheet and cover my bottom? This situation is really quite embarrassing."

"I don't think I should do that, Oliver," said Bernard, who was happy to see Oliver's predicament prolonged. "I'm sure the medical student knew what he was doing. Perhaps the fresh air will help your wound."

Bernard succumbed to his morbid curiosity and leaned forward to take a closer look at Oliver's derriere. Surrounding an area of missing tissue were the impressions that had been left by Napoleon's two rows of teeth. An angry wound to say the least.

"But—"

"I'll be right back, Oliver."

As Bernard stepped through the curtain, he was confronted by a wall of white coats. The doctors stepped past him wordlessly and surrounded Oliver's bed. Bernard remained inside the curtain, curious to see the outcome of Oliver's examination.

Radiating a self-satisfied air, the attending physician stood at the center of a group of residents and medical students. The physician was Ballwinder Singh, and he was the Director of the Division of Proctologic Surgery at Vengeful Savior. Bernard recalled that Dr. Singh had been the honored recipient of the Melchior P. Thwaite Award at the annual benefit of the Schistosomiasis Society at Morningwood, although due to his dusky complexion he had been required to enter and exit the club by a side door.

The Schistosomiasis Society had presented a moving video montage of Dr. Singh's career, with a particular emphasis on his early years when he had become engaged in a noble but ultimately unsuccessful effort to quell an epidemic of gastrointestinal disorders by fencing off the Ganges River to prevent the people of Calcutta from drinking from and bathing and relieving themselves in its squalid waters. Although certain of the graphic images in the video had caused many of the club members to lose their appetite and a few to rush off to the restrooms, there could be no doubt that Dr. Singh had come far in the world.

Bernard looked on as Dr. Singh began. "Gentlemen," he said, which resulted in looks of annoyance from the women in the group, "today we have a very interesting case: a man with a bite to the buttock."

"Excuse me?" said Oliver.

"What makes this case interesting?" continued Dr. Singh, ignoring Oliver. "Anyone?"

"Excuse me?" repeated Oliver in a slightly louder voice.

"What is this interruption?" asked Dr. Singh with annoyance.

"Well, I'm the fellow with the bite to his buttock," responded Oliver in an ingratiating tone, "and I was wondering if you might be able to take me down from this hoist. I believe that I could lie in exactly the same position on the mattress."

"Sir, your turn will come, but at present I am addressing the students. Please do not interrupt me again."

"But—"

"Sedatives!" cried Ballwinder Singh.

"Yes, Dr. Singh," answered the senior resident, who stepped forward holding a large syringe.

"Alright, alright, I won't say another word, I promise!" pleaded Oliver. The resident waited for Dr. Singh's response with the syringe held aloft.

"Fine. I will continue. But I will have you sedated if you continue to disrupt my didactics. Now, I was asking a question. What makes this case interesting?"

"The unusual arrangement of teeth for a human bite?" offered a resident.

"It was a dog bite," said Oliver defensively.

"Silence!" warned Dr. Singh. "But, as the patient states, it was a dog bite, so the pattern of teeth marks is appropriate. Anyone else?"

"The amount of tissue that was bitten away?" asked one of the medical students, prompting Oliver to wonder whether it might be possible to have a prosthetic buttock fabricated.

"No, given that this patient is morbidly obese, it is not surprising that the beast was able to grab hold of and tear off a chunk the size of a golf ball. Anyone else?"

Oliver did not appreciate being characterized as morbidly obese, but he said nothing.

"No one else?" said Dr. Singh. "Alright, the interesting aspect of this case is—"

"Excuse me, please allow me to pass."

In this instance, Oliver was not the source of the interruption, although he was concerned that Dr. Singh might have him sedated anyway. Instead, Margaret Van Buren was pushing her way through the group of doctors to Oliver's bedside. Ballwinder Singh recognized her immediately.

"Why, Mrs. Van Buren, it's a pleasure to see you, as always, but these are, er, such *unusual* circumstances," he said, gesturing toward the bitten buttock. Oliver plummeted through the depths of embarrassment into a state of utter mortification.

"Yes, Dr. Singh, how are you? Well, I'm not here to see you; I'm here to see your patient. At least the front of him. Well, the upper part of the front of him, hopefully."

"Greetings, Mrs. Van Buren," said Oliver to Luis and Carlotta. "I regret that you are seeing me in this unfortunate state. I had a bit of a mishap with my beloved pet. He tried to give me a playful nip and apparently he went too far."

"Yes, quite a bit too far," said Mrs. Van Buren, inspecting Oliver's rear. "Mr. Booth, although I don't mean to neglect your unfortunate injury, I am desperate to find my grandson Martin. My housekeeper was supposed to pick him up at school yesterday, but he wasn't there. I called everyone, including the police, and I didn't know where to turn until I saw you on television earlier today, with Bernard and Martin, when you caused that riot. Do you have any idea where they are now?"

"Mrs. Van Buren, I'm right here," said Bernard, stepping forward through the group of doctors, "and Martin is right outside. I stopped by your house yesterday to speak with you after we returned from Paris and I found Martin waiting in the backyard. He has been safe with me ever since. I'm so relieved to see you. Where have you been?"

"I was in New York to attend an auction at Sotheby's. I had spoken with my housekeeper at length, Bernard, and she fully understood that I would be away for a short time but available by telephone. I can't imagine what must have happened. She's usually so reliable."

"Martin told me that he had been dropped off at your house at noon by the school bus. He said that school ended early because the teachers had a meeting. Had you told him that your housekeeper would be picking him up?"

Mrs. Van Buren paused to think. "Yes, I did, but I hadn't known that the students would be released so early. When he didn't see her, he probably just took the school bus home like he does every other day."

"And I found him and led him off to look for you before your housekeeper could explain the situation," said Bernard. "I guess it was just a simple misunderstanding. Or maybe not so simple."

"Not so simple at all, Bernard, not so simple at all," said Mrs. Van Buren. "But thank God Martin is safe, and thank you for looking after him. I hope he wasn't too much trouble?"

"Actually, it was quite a challenge to be responsible for Martin. I don't know how you do it."

"Why do you think I sometimes ask my housekeeper to help me, Bernard? It's not due to *my* age, it's due to *his*."

"Mrs. Van Buren, I hope I'm not being rude by asking you this, but why does Martin live with you? Where are his parents?"

"That's certainly a reasonable question, Bernard, particularly after everything that has happened." Mrs. Van Buren paused to take a deep breath and then continued. "My daughter Monique, Martin's mother, had a bit of a fling with one of my gardeners when she was 18. His name was Raul, and he looked a bit like Che Guevara. He even wore a beret. You know how 18-year-old girls can be."

"Not really," said Bernard, betraying the ignorance of the single man.

"Anyway, one thing led to another, and ten months later we had Martin. Well, she had Martin, but she was only 18, and in her own way she was still a baby, so I told her that I would take responsibility for him while she completed her education.

She's 28 now and she's finishing her studies at the London School of Economics. I suppose I've been more of a mother to Martin than she has, but they seem to have a good relationship. He treats her more like an older sister than a mother, which means that he abuses her like the rest of us. In his heart he's a good boy, though."

"Don't tell him I said so, but I think you're right," said Bernard.

"Excuse me, I hate to interrupt your little heart-to-heart, but I'm still here!" said Oliver, now feeling more ignored than embarrassed. Bernard and Mrs. Van Buren turned to find that Dr. Singh and his group of trainees had also been listening raptly to their entire conversation.

"Yes, Mr. Booth, I noticed," said Mrs. Van Buren. "I wish you well, but I must go and see my grandson. Doctor, when do you expect that you will be discharging Mr. Booth?"

"In my expert opinion, I anticipate that we will be sending him home within the hour," responded Dr. Singh. "A few stitches and some pills and he'll be as good as new! Missing a bit of his butt, of course, but he could stand to lose a few pounds. Couldn't you, Mr. Booth?"

Oliver sighed as the group roared with laughter.

Dr. Singh continued. "Now, Mrs. Van Buren, I am so pleased that your good friend Mr. Booth is out of the woods, as you laypeople like to say, thanks to my expert intervention. Please allow me, then, to ask you a question. Have you ever thought of extending your philanthropic endeavors to Vengeful Savior? We were hoping to build a new plastic-surgery wing to provide services to our friends from Palm Beach, but construction can be so expensive."

"How much money will it cost?" asked Mrs. Van Buren, suspicious of Dr. Singh's intentions.

Eagerly, the doctor responded, "Ten million dollars?"

"Unlikely."

"Five million dollars would still go a long way."

"I don't think so."

"Perhaps naming us in your will—"

"Dr. Singh, I anticipate that my unfortunate demise will be many years in the future," she responded with finality.

Mrs. Van Buren turned away from Dr. Singh and spoke directly to Oliver's buttocks. "Mr. Booth, since you will be discharged within the hour, I would appreciate it if you would be at my home tomorrow morning at 9:00. I would like to meet with you and Bernard to review your purchases. We're going to go over my guesthouse from top to . . . bottom?"

Mrs. Van Buren was laughing as she and Bernard left Oliver's room to find Martin.

Chapter Fourteen

Oliver slept fitfully that night after having been discharged from Vengeful Savior. Dr. Singh, perhaps in a final act of retribution for Oliver's uncooperative behavior, had suggested that he purchase an over-the-counter analgesic to help him cope with the persistent throbbing pain in his buttock, and he had refused to heed his patient's pleas for something just a little bit stronger. Despite his constant tossing and turning, Oliver had been unable to find a position that would permit him to lapse into unconsciousness, and it was only as the sun rose that he realized that the traction apparatus had actually made some sense after all.

Oliver had called for a taxi to take him to Mrs. Van Buren's house, and he had been dismayed to see a ramshackle Chevy from the early 1970s roll up outside his door. He felt every bump during the short ride, and he stepped out of the car with a grimace, refusing to offer the driver a tip. He pulled on the entry gong at the front door and was greeted by James, who escorted him to the living room, where Bernard and Mrs. Van Buren were already waiting.

"Good morning, Mr. Booth," said Mrs. Van Buren, "I trust you had a restful night?"

"Unfortunately, no, I didn't sleep at all. I couldn't find a comfortable position."

"You poor man, you must be exhausted. I'll have James bring you some coffee. Please, sit down."

"Thank you, Mrs. Van Buren, but I don't think coffee would make any difference at this point. I wonder, though, could I trouble you for a small pillow? I'm finding it difficult to sit for extended periods without extra cushioning."

"Certainly, Mr. Booth. I will get you one myself."

Mrs. Van Buren stood up and walked across the room, where she found a pillow elaborately decorated in silk brocade. She brought it back to Oliver, who positioned it under his buttock and sat down gingerly.

Mrs. Van Buren opened their meeting. "Now, Mr. Booth, Bernard and I were just about to begin discussing your shopping expedition. As leader of the expedition, it is your prerogative to present a summary of your successes."

Oliver brightened, believing that his merits were finally being recognized, and said, "Absolutely, Mrs. Van Buren, absolutely!" He reached into his jacket pocket and withdrew two sheets of paper. "I have taken the liberty of extracting the rel-evant information from all of those complicated invoices and summarizing them on these sheets. Here you will find a description of every item that I purchased, the price that I negotiated, and the total price for all of my purchases at the bottom. If you find that to be satisfactory, you can make out a check to me, Oliver Booth, and I will wire the money to the shipping company as soon as it clears."

"But I'm confused, Mr. Booth. Why would I write a check to you if I could just wire the money to the shipping company directly? I would then receive my furniture that much more quickly. What is the total amount? I will call my private banker and have it done immediately."

Oliver panicked. "Oh no, Mrs. Van Buren, please allow me to be your intermediary. All you need to do is write one little check and allow me to take it from there. I don't want you to be bothered by any complicated financial arrangements." Oliver knew that if Mrs. Van Buren wired the total amount of money he had requested, the shipping company would alert her banker that it was far in excess of what she actually owed.

"Well, perhaps you're right. I may be acting in too hasty a fashion. Why don't we review your summary sheets?"

"Absolutely, Mrs. Van Buren. By the way, may I call you Margaret?"

"No."

Bernard smiled as Oliver loosened his collar prior to beginning his presentation. "Um, alright. So! Item number one. A Louis the Fifteenth commode, price $5,000." Oliver looked up to find Bernard and Mrs. Van Buren staring at him. He continued. "Item number two, a Louis the Fourteenth se-manier, price $8,250." Still no response. "Alright, item number three, a Louis the Fifteenth *bergère*, price $5,300. Aren't you going to say anything? These items sound quite impressive, don't they?"

"I'm not sure what to say, Mr. Booth. For whom did you purchase these items? Certainly not for me."

"What do you mean? Of course all of these items were purchased for you."

Mrs. Van Buren picked up a folder that was lying on the coffee table in front of her. "But my dear Mr. Booth, I have here copies of all of the original invoices that the shipping company faxed to me soon after your return. The items you described are not listed on these invoices. Look, for example, item number one, a Napoleon the Third commode, price 2,000 Euros. Item number two, a Louis the Fifteenth semanier, price 3,500 Euros. Item number three, a Napoleon the Third bergère, price 1,900 Euros. And one particular item caught my eye, an oil painting of Saint Gisella. Who on earth is Saint Gisella? I could go on, Mr. Booth. Shall I? Or would you like to continue?"

He had been set up. Oliver fumed. Only Bernard had known his plan. He would get him for this. "That won't be necessary," he said.

"Mr. Booth, I really do believe in the inherent goodness of people, so I had decided to give you one last chance to be honest with me this morning. Obviously, my intentions were misguided. By my rough calculations, the total cost stated on your so-called summary sheets exceeds the real cost of your shopping expedition by approximately $400,000. How do you explain that?"

Oliver remained silent, sulking.

"You can't explain it, other than to admit to fraud." Mrs. Van Buren reached down and picked up a bell from the coffee table to summon her butler. "James, please call the police. I would like to report a crime."

"Yes, ma'am," said James, "with pleasure!" He scowled at Oliver and turned to leave.

"No, Mrs. Van Buren, please, this will destroy my reputation!" implored Oliver. "Reputation is everything in antiques! I'll have no future in Palm Beach!"

"Mr. Booth, you can't destroy something that doesn't exist. Perhaps your future will be in West Palm Beach. In jail."

"Please! I'll do anything, anything!" he begged, weeping.

"Anything?"

"Anything!"

"Alright. First, you are several months past due in paying the rent on your shop. That amounts to $13,500. You will repay that debt immediately."

"But how do you know about that? Why do you care about my rent?" Oliver paused, recognizing that he was in no position to negotiate. "Yes, of course, I can assure you that I will pay my rent as soon as I return to my shop."

"Mr. Booth, I used the word '*immediately*' and that means now. The reason I am interested in your rent is because *I* am your landlord. You might recall that your space is owned by VB Holdings? Have you ever wondered what the VB stands for?"

"Van Buren?" replied Oliver in a meek voice.

"Very good, Mr. Booth! Now, as I said, you owe me $13,500. Your payment, please." Mrs. Van Buren extended her hand and waited expectantly.

Oliver reached slowly into his jacket pocket and withdrew a thick envelope filled with $100 bills. He began counting.

"Why, Mr. Booth, the antique business has been good to you, hasn't it? Where did you get all of that money?"

"Oh, a deal here, a deal there," mumbled Oliver.

"That isn't the money you took from those poor unfortunates who came to pray to your bogus Saint Gisella, is it?"

Oliver's eyes widened. "You know about that too?" he asked.

"Yes, now give me that envelope if you don't want me to bring a second charge of fraud against you." Oliver handed her the envelope. "I will see that this money is donated to dermatologic research. That's a much more appropriate use of this money than trying to curry favor with that ridiculous so-called saint."

Mrs. Van Buren passed the envelope to James. "That still leaves the matter of your unpaid rent, Mr. Booth."

"But I don't have any more money, Mrs. Van Buren. The well has run dry."

Mrs. Van Buren nodded to James, who walked over to Oliver with some papers and a pen.

"Mr. Booth, the legal document that you have been handed, and will sign, acknowledges that you are giving up the lease on your shop due to the nonpayment of rent. You are no longer the proprietor of the shop. You further acknowledge that the goods in the shop, as tacky as they may be, are now my property and that their somewhat limited value will serve as partial payment of your past-due rent."

"Now see here," began Oliver.

"No, you see here, Mr. Booth," interjected Mrs. Van Buren. "You have a simple choice. Accept this plan or prepare for the arrival of the police. Jail can be quite an unpleasant place, I hear. Particularly for those with a delicate disposition."

Oliver self-consciously adjusted the position of his buttock on the silk cushion. "Alright, I'll sign the papers," he said, eyes cast downward.

"Second, Mr. Booth, you will seek alternative employment, and you will pay me $500 every month until the remainder of your debt is satisfied."

"But Mrs. Van Buren, where will I be able to find work? A man like myself, of a certain age? Who would hire me?"

"Funny you should mention that, Mr. Booth. I think I can be of service. Would you like a position in one of my companies?"

"After all this you would offer me a job? Yes, of course, I would be so grateful."

"Fine," said Mrs. Van Buren. She turned to face Bernard. "I know I haven't spoken with you about this, Bernard, but I want to show you how much I appreciate your good work for me over in Paris, as well as your honesty. And I know Martin would never tell you this himself, but he adores you. He mentioned that as he was about to leave for school this morning. Tell me, Bernard, do you remember the first time we met? I purchased that commode you had acquired at an estate sale? Over Mr. Booth's protests?"

"Of course."

"Well, perhaps I knew something that you didn't, but your instincts were remarkable. I also did a little research. That commode—actually, it would be more accurately described as a *table en bureau*, like a writing table with drawers, but that's neither here nor there—was fabricated by André-Charles Boulle around 1710, or during the period of Louis the Fourteenth. Boulle was the official cabinetmaker to the king, and he developed a technique involving the inlay of tortoiseshell and brass that is now known as Boulle marquetry. During the second half of the 18th century, the piece was acquired by the Comte de Vaudreuil, a member of Marie Antoinette's inner circle, who had it modified according to the conventions of the period by Cuvellier, a gifted restorer about whom little is known. Sotheby's recently auctioned a virtually identical piece for $1,688,000, and it had been thought at the time to be one of a kind. Apparently not."

Bernard was shocked. "$1,688,000? That's ridiculous. I mean, it's quite an impressive piece, but—"

"Bernard," interrupted Mrs. Van Buren, "the craftsmanship is irreproachable, and Boulle is a historically important cabinetmaker. Hence, the price. Now I'm sure you'll remember that I told you that my ill-timed disappearance from Palm Beach was because of my attendance at an auction at Sotheby's in New York. What I didn't tell you was that the item being auctioned was your . . . actually my . . . commode. I did love that piece, Bernard, but you were right when you said that $1,688,000 was a ridiculous amount of money to pay for a piece of furniture. So I decided to auction it off in the hope of obtaining an equally ridiculous amount of money that I could use for a better purpose."

"What was the winning bid?" asked Bernard with excitement.

"Well, Bernard, remember that the first piece was far more valuable because it was thought to be one of a kind," responded Mrs. Van Buren coyly. With a mock frown, she said, "I'm sorry to tell you that your piece sold for only $1,270,000. I hope you're not disappointed."

Bernard was stunned.

"I can't believe that the auctioneer at the estate sale didn't realize the importance of the piece," continued Mrs. Van Buren, "but it was lucky for you that he didn't. Perhaps he thought it was a Napoleon the Third reproduction. When I reviewed the shipper's invoices and the photographs of the items you purchased in Paris, Bernard, it just confirmed my feelings about your abilities. Thus, I hope you will accept my offer to become the manager of my new antique shop."

"But that's *my* job! He's just a waiter!" interjected Oliver in outrage.

"Not anymore. The shop—and the apartment, by the way—is no longer yours, Mr. Booth, and Bernard is no longer a waiter. Unless, of course, he would prefer to remain a waiter. Would you, Bernard?" asked Mrs. Van Buren, smiling.

"Well, I'm shocked, Mrs. Van Buren. I don't know what to say," responded Bernard with a dazed look.

"Please begin by calling me Margaret and end by accepting my offer."

"Well, of course I will accept your offer, but I'm not sure that I will be very successful selling the goods that are in the shop now."

"That junk? Donate it to a charity. I could use a tax deduction. Here," she said, handing Bernard a check.

"What's this?" he asked.

"A check for $1 million. Essentially, that is the profit I obtained by selling the commode at Sotheby's, minus the seller's commission and other fees. I'm giving you those funds as an investment in the shop."

Bernard was stunned. "This is so generous, I don't know what to say."

"Perhaps you should book another trip to Paris. You now have a store to fill!"

"But where does this leave me?" asked Oliver.

"Mr. Booth, I mentioned that I would employ you in one of my companies, and I will do exactly that," said Mrs. Van Buren. "You will be Bernard's new clerk."

"Absolutely not! I would never—"

"James, have the police arrived yet?" she shouted, smiling.

"Alright, alright," said Oliver. "I'll do whatever is necessary to pay back the rent. I don't want to go to jail."

"And I think it's only fair that you repay me for the expenses you accrued on your trip to Paris, don't you agree, Mr.

Booth? I mean, you really weren't acting in my service, so I don't think I should have to pay for all of your massages and pedicures."

"You know about those?"

"Yes."

"Alright, I'll repay the trip expenses too."

"Finally, Bernard, I have a gift for you on the occasion of the beginning of your new business venture," said Mrs. Van Buren as she handed him a package.

"What is it?" he asked.

"Take a look," she said.

Bernard unwrapped the package and began to laugh.

"What is it?" asked Oliver.

Bernard turned and showed him the gift. It was a framed clipping from the front page of the *Shiny Sheet* showing Oliver being carried out of the flea market on a stretcher with Madame Barbelé in hot pursuit.

Oliver groaned.

"What a wonderful gift, Margaret," said Bernard with a twinkle in his eye. "I will hang it in a place of honor." He turned to face his new clerk. "Now, Oliver, I believe that it is time for us to return to the shop. We have a great deal of work ahead of us before we will be able to reopen. First, you will schedule the Salvation Army to pick up all of the goods that are currently on display. Please tell them we will need their largest truck. Second, to continue the tradition that you established, you will then stand and present me with my mail. I anticipate there will be many bills that are well past due, and subscriptions to certain popular magazines will need to be canceled. Third, you will assist me in organizing another trip to Paris."

"Oh goody!" said Oliver. "When will we be leaving?"

"*'We'* are not leaving. *I* will be traveling alone. Is that understood?"

"Yes, Bernard."

"Excuse me? What did you call me?"

"I mean yes, Mr. Dauphin."

"Better, Oliver, much better," said Bernard. "I'm beginning to think you might have potential!"

EPILOGUE

As the social season wound down, the residents of Palm Beach continued to partake of their favorite amusements, oblivious—for the most part—to the small intrigues described in these pages. Trophy wives shopped, their wealthy husbands had affairs, and everyone had aesthetic reconstruction. As an equatorial climate crept north, residents began their seasonal migration to their summer homes in the Hamptons and Newport, followed by a phalanx of waiters in hot pursuit of temporary jobs and further gratuities. In the off-season, the population of the island tends to be overwhelmingly composed of the staff members who maintain the homes of their affluent employers, scrubbing floors, replacing lightbulbs, and sorting and perhaps perusing the mail that is always one step behind its intended recipients. Those families that choose to remain on the island miss out on the succession of gala events held up north, but perhaps just a few of them like it that way.

Worth Avenue is vacant in the summer, and shopkeepers spend most of their time gazing blankly out of their windows into the harsh sunlight reflecting off the asphalt road. Oliver and Bernard were now among them, and they had somehow found a way to coexist within the narrow confines of Le Magasin du Dauphin, as Bernard had renamed the shop. Perhaps Oliver had even taken a small amount of fatherly pride in Bernard's rapid success, but more likely not.

Each believed that he was the rightful proprietor of the shop, but only Bernard had been able to turn a profit. His approach had been simple. In such a small space, he had decided that he would display only a limited selection of items of absolutely impeccable beauty and provenance, and he offered them to the public at a fair price. In that way, and facilitated by the frequent recommendations of Mrs. Van Buren, he had developed a devoted clientele in just a few short months, and it was the volume of their purchases rather than the profits that he accrued on individual items that had made Bernard a success. A shop off Worth Avenue had become a destination after all.

Bernard was a highly professional merchant, and his constant attendance during the hours that his shop was open left his clerk with little to do. Oliver had fleeting opportunities to recapture his past glory when Bernard would leave to play soccer with Martin every afternoon, but he had no chance for mischief because after he returned, Bernard would inspect the limited inventory and review any transactions that might have occurred.

When his shop was closed, Bernard had become devoted to a new endeavor. Monique Van Buren had completed her studies at the London School of Economics, you see, and she had decided to move to Palm Beach to be closer to her son.

With Mrs. Van Buren's gentle encouragement, a romance had quickly grown between the former waiter with the cute accent and the slightly older woman with a Che Guevara fixation. Martin couldn't help but roll his eyes whenever he saw them together, but in his heart he could not have been happier.

ACKNOWLEDGMENTS

Writing is a solitary activity, but a writer depends upon many other people throughout that process. Darcie Rowan and Meg McAllister of the McAllister Rowan Communications Group have provided indispensable advice regarding the production and marketing of this book. Similarly, the expertise and careful attention of the team at the Greenleaf Book Group have been much appreciated. I would also like to thank the many people who graciously permitted me to add their endorsements to this book and the press materials.

On a personal note, I would like to acknowledge my family, and in particular my mother, who taught me that ambition and perseverance can make any goal attainable. This book is dedicated to my wife Lisa and my son Robert, whose wholehearted support made its completion possible.

David Desmond
Palm Beach, Florida

ABOUT THE AUTHOR

Born in New York City, David Desmond is the grandson of famed real estate developer Fred Trump, the nephew of the celebrated entrepreneur Donald Trump, and the son of Judge Maryanne Trump Barry of the United States Court of Appeals for the Third Circuit. He is a graduate of the University of Chicago with a degree in the Behavioral Sciences and received his Master's and Ph.D. in Clinical Psychology from Fordham University. Currently, David resides in Palm Beach and Paris with his wife and their son. He is finishing his second novel, which will follow the continuing adventures of Oliver Booth in the world of real estate in Palm Beach and Manhattan.

PERSONAL APPEARANCES

David Desmond welcomes book club and reading festival invitations. Please contact him at daviddesmond@dlrd.net or visit www.oliverbooth.com for more information.